588882

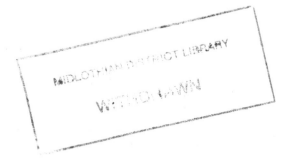
20p

A GAME OF DARK

A Game of Dark
William Mayne

HAMISH HAMILTON

Printed in Great Britain by
Western Printing Services Ltd, Bristol

TO KATHARINE DICKSON

I

DONALD HEARD MR SAVERY shouting at him: "Jackson,
what's the matter?" Donald tried to speak, but he had no
throat to speak with and nothing to say, nothing that he knew
about.

Then, in a little while (something like half an hour later,
his eyes told him, while Mr Savery stared at him and the board
duster folded slowly into a restful heap, falling liquidly from
Mr Savery's hand and leaving its own shadow in the air, made
of chalk dust) a voice spoke for him, not out of his mouth, but
from just above his head, but he knew it was himself speaking.
"I feel sick," said this spokesman.

"You'd better go out," said Mr Savery, oozing forwards
from his place by the board and stretching out a hand to take
Donald's arm. The chalk dust ghost of the duster swirled
angrily round the moving arm. Donald heard the voices coming
more quickly now, and more clearly, over the things that had
been happening just before they spoke and appeared in his
sight. The next to speak was Nessing, who got up from beside
Donald, who was startled to see him because he had only
been seeing things straight ahead of him, like Mr Savery at
the end of a tunnel of existence, a bright distinctness seen
through a shadow. "I'll take him out," said Nessing, and he
laid a disappointing hand on Donald's shoulder.

7

With that touch Donald was truly back in his own class-room. He knew that should have been a comfort to him, but it was not. He knew he should have been in a much worse place, and had been there, and there was still a silence and was still a sound from that other place in his head. Only from his eyes had the vision cleared.

He was standing up, he found. He was either very cold, or the classroom was very hot. For the moment he did not know. His limbs, and particularly his neck, felt very stiff. In his mouth and nostrils and throat there was a stench, metallic and rotten and piercing, the most foul he had ever known, and that was the worst thing and what made him feel so sick. It made him worse than sick, though: the stench was not only felt by the ordinary senses of taste and smell but sensed by the whole of his skin, and seemed to weigh in every bone. Donald was astonished that the whole room did not cry out against him, because a smell like this on him should have brought protest from everyone.

He had brought it with him, he knew. Now it began to fade from him, and with it faded the memory of where he had been. As Nessing led him from the room, as Mr Savery's voice began again behind them, the fading went on, until there was hardly anything left but the memory of the stench (more like having a strange shape in the mouth than a strange gas), the remembrance of a cry in darkness from some un-known person, and a sense of urgency, something to be done as soon as possible.

"Take him to the staff lavatory," was what Mr Savery said.

"Girls' bog is nearest," said Nessing quietly to Donald, and showed an inclination, for a moment, to turn left towards

8

them. Donald resisted slightly, and Nessing let him walk straight ahead, and Donald let him lead now. They went through the staff sitting room, the quickest way to the staff lavatory.

"Here we are," said Nessing, stopping in the middle of the staff room. "Puke on the carpet if you're going to."

"Not going to," said Donald, with his own voice this time and not the spokesman. "It's gone away. What happened?"

"Not much," said Nessing. "Go on, have a little puke, they can't blame you, what an opportunity, it wouldn't half upset them."

"Oh, shut up," said Donald. "I told you I didn't feel sick any more. What happened?"

"I think I'll get your Mum," said Nessing. "Sit down." Donald sat down. Nessing went out of the room. He was full of contradiction between declaration and behaviour. He was the enemy of all members of staff, considered as authority, yet at the funeral of little and very old Mrs Lesley, which he had not been made to attend by any means and which had taken place during the holidays, he had been seen in tears. Last winter, on the day of deepest snow, he had spent four hours digging out the headmaster's drive anonymously, while the headmaster was away but expected back that night. Now he had urged Donald to befoul the staff room, and then gone, full of care for his patient, to another class to fetch Donald's mother.

The passages of school were quiet for a moment. Farthest off were the timpani of the table layers in the hall, ringing the chrome-steel sounds of cutlery. Schools were for learning, Donald thought, not for eating in, which was an impurity of function. But he did not feel hungry.

9

There was a nearer noise. Nessing tapping a door and opening it, the escape of a roll of sound from the snare of the room beyond, and the closing of the door barring the noise again. Then the door opened again, letting out that background sound of a classroom you might judge silent from within because you are used to the moving of feet and the expansion and contraction of lungs and the chafing of clothes and the ploughing of pens into unexplored paper. Above that usual background came his mother's voice, saying something about the Central Asian Plateau and Crustal Folds. She and Nessing came back to the staff room.

"You can go back to your lesson, Nessing," she said.

"Yes, Mrs Jackson," said Nessing.

"And thank you for coming for me; it was sensible," she said.

Nessing went. "Now, Jackson, what's the matter?" said his mother. She called him Jackson in school, and he called her Mrs Jackson, and of course the same thing very often at home.

"I felt sick," said Donald. "And strange."

"How do you feel now?" said Mrs Jackson. "Have you been sick?"

"I feel funny but all right," said Donald. "I don't think I'll be sick now."

"You look a bit pale still," said Mrs Jackson. "Stay here for the rest of the lesson, and we'll see how you are at dinner time." She put a hand that was part motherly and part schoolteacherly on his forehead, and he felt it partly as a son and partly as a pupil, stiffening his neck only a little. She left him and went back to the Crustal Folds of the Siberian Plateau. Donald sat on a chair with his back to the window. The bright light of the rainy September day bothered him, and the greenness of the grass and trees, and the low horizon of the sea that brought the sky to below eye level and even where horizon began reflected below it as brightly again, silver and still at a distance, in spite of the cloud flying low from the land.

There was a last unison crash from the performer in the dining hall, then the diminuendo whickering of a swing door, and quiet from there. Now there was only the pushing of the wind outdoors. Donald sat in the vacuum of indoors and heard the weather being pumped past, as if it were emptying the building and increasing the internal vacuum.

Donald found that his memory of another place, where he had seemed to be before he heard Mr Savery's voice asking him what was the matter, that memory, overpowering and in-distinct as it was then, had gone far away, like the line between sky and sea, but become more distinct and factual. Donald shaded his eyes and looked from the window, not at the horizon, but as a check on the sort of actuality out there. There was no help to memory there. He had slippery distant facts, real ones, in mind. The shout, the urgency, the—he could hardly remem-ber and he wondered if he imagined it—girl who had cried out and needed help. Was it real, or a dream, or a fancy, or a wish? Was it the girl in the picture?

Before he could think about the picture, which was at home, the door of the school opened and weather came in, and after the weather a tread that Donald knew well and that pleased him. It was Mr Braxham, the vicar, who came to school dinner on Tuesdays and took classes afterwards. He came into the staff room swinging his cloak and his black hat, one round his shoulders and the other in his hand.

"Hello, Berry," said Donald. Berry was what Mr Braxham liked to be called.

"Donald," said Mr Braxham, "what's up? You look pretty bloody. Is there a row on?"

"No," said Donald. "I just felt a bit sick."

"Your belly isn't my concern," said Mr Braxham, "and it isn't a matter of conscience, I suppose; but bless you in any case, even though you are a Methodist, and like St Paul I recommend a little wine for the stomach's sake. Do you mind if I smoke? The next best thing to wine, I suppose."

He lit a cigarette, then dropped his hat under a chair, threw his cloak over it and said he would go and wash his hands before going down to the kitchen to see what was for dinner. He went off to the staff lavatory, leaving his burning cigarette in the ashtray. Donald knew it was left for him to have a drag at if he wanted. He watched the smoke roping up into the air. The staff lavatory gurgled and Mr Braxham came out. He picked up his undisturbed cigarette and sucked smoke from it. Then he handed it to Donald.

"I don't smoke, you know, Berry," said Donald.

"All the better," said Mr Brixham. "It'll do you more good to have a couple of puffs. It's a drug, you know, like alcohol. You take two puffs, that's the recommended dose today. Go on, take it in, right in."

Donald had smoked several times, and made himself dizzy once and had not tried again. Now he trusted Mr Braxham to know what was good for him, and took the cigarette. He pulled smoke into his mouth and then into his throat and then further down still, and the smoke melted away under his ribs and came out dry from his mouth.

12

"Again," said Mr Braxham. Donald did it again, and then handed the cigarette back. Mr Braxham's face came closer when he bent over for the cigarette. There was rain still wet on his broad red cheek and on the full flesh between chin and neck, before the white collar gathered all the skin into itself.

"I'll go down to the kitchen now," he said. "You sit here and relax; you're too tense."

"Twenty," said Donald, but two tense are twenty was not Berry's kind of joke, he thought, and if he explained it Berry would laugh out of duty and Donald would feel he was doing it so that he did not hurt Donald's feelings, and Donald did not want to put him in that position, bringing something between them. As it was he could not see him without realizing that very soon, in a matter of weeks, Mr Braxham was leaving the parish for another appointment. Then Mr Braxham went off down the passage, leaving Donald alone with smoke in him and a heart that longed for Berry to be staying and talking to him and noticing him.

Yet there was something that Donald wanted to be left alone with: his memory of the moments before leaving the class room. It had been an ordinary mathematics lesson, dealing with the theory of indices. Then it had been something else. Donald leaned back and thought of it, and felt two waves of change flow through his muscles and a certain tightness fall from his cheeks and wrists. He licked his lips, that were bitter with tobacco.

What had happened? Had it been only a dream? Had a girl shouted for him? What had been the urgency? Cold air fell from the window behind him, and he remembered another cold that had been on him, not long ago, and yet unreachably distant. He leaned back, alone in the staff room, and touched the beaded line of memory, shrinking from the electricity in the touching, the nerve of fear that sent the current through him as he explored.

His mind touched the problem, then left it, and wandered. He did not know where it had gone. Then he was almost in two places at once, or perhaps in a place from which he could step into either of two worlds. One was a hillside of green bracken and small trees, cold and grey, and the other was that small room called the staff room, heavy with polish and smoke and use but empty. The hillside was not quite empty; he knew there was someone in it somewhere, who needed help, and was in great fear for an unknown but understandable reason.

There was twilight. He looked back over the morning, while he had been walking southwards down the coast, and wondered why the night was drawing close when the sun was still high. But he had thought that once, and more than once, he knew, and he had wondered why it was cold over this crest of the hill, so cold in this autumn day that his foot had slid on ice. He knew that something had interrupted what he was doing. He found he was holding his breath, and he breathed in, unlocking his nostrils to do so. They had been wrinkled up. There was a powerful and terrible smell, like nothing known to him before, that filled his throat and made him gag and then bend over and vomit. Then that was over, and he was not quite so aware of the smell hanging in the still air. When he had stopped hearing his own body writhing, and had spat and spat and dashed tears from his eyes, part from the convulsions of his throat and part from the bitterness of the smoky smell, he could hear other noises. He turned round, and saw

14

the girl. She was lying on the cold ground, spread out help-lessly, and she was moaning and gasping for breath. He did not know who she was, or what she was doing here, but he was not surprised at that, because he was the stranger who had wandered here. The girl had been sick too and had not been able to get up and move away. He had seen her once already, he knew, before the stench had overcome him, the stench that rose from the whole of the ground round him, where it was torn and crushed in a broad band like a track, marked across the hillside through the broken trees and tramped bracken. Over all the green, over the gouged marks in the earth, lay the frozen slime from which the stench came. He stood in it with bare feet. The girl lay in it, dressed in a woollen shift the same colour as a sheep. She tried to raise herself, but she shook too much with cold and fear so that she had not enough control to crawl. He bent to her and put an arm under her shoulder and lifted her up and she stood for a moment before folding again from the waist. He thought of taking her up the hill into the untouched grassy slopes where there was more sunshine, northwards, but she resisted with her weight and straightened a little, trying to walk down the hill, over the broad band of desolation and nastiness.

She spoke, but he did not try to hear the words. He let her weight rest on him and helped her over the ruts and hillocks. All the time he grew colder until his own legs were shaking. The girl grew stronger as they went, but had to be supported all the way. Then they were over the vile ice and walking on a clean hillside in the mist, and the ground was warmer and so was the air. The stench grew less, but they had brought it with them, and it still hung upon them.

15

They walked down and down. He looked back and saw the track on the hill laid like a contour line, but narrower now. All was silent, nothing moved in the mist except their own bare feet shifting the grass and their own broken breathing, because the stench had roughened their throats and the cold air and mist caught there and pricked in their lungs too.

A noise came, of running water, and ahead there was a little stream. The girl said something, but again he did not want to listen and understand, without knowing why. They walked towards the water, and then drew away from it. It had come from higher up the hill, as they had, and like them it had brought down with it the foulness from above. But to go where the girl wanted to go they had to cross it, and they jumped it without touching it, and fell coughing on the far bank because the exertion jerked their sore lungs.

The next water they came to was a clean pond, still and reflecting the steady twilight above and around. In it they walked and replaced the slime with sandy mud that did not smell, and washed their hands and the girl washed her face. Then they walked to the other side and rinsed their mouths free, spitting the water on the bank and then drinking. The girl sat down and rubbed her shift with the rough-grown autumn grass. Then she looked at him and spoke.

"Carrica," she said.

He did not want to understand or hear what she said. He knew that he could find out what she meant, what the word was, if he thought about it, but to think about it was too disturbing. He let it be a word, a sound, and left it at that. He smiled instead of replying. She spoke again, more words that he did not dare to assimilate and digest. If he did let himself think of meanings he found some other thought and place pressing on him, bringing such discomfort that he could not bear it. He smiled again, and stood up. The girl still sat where she was, looking at him and waiting for him to understand. She repeated her words. This time he had to allow himself to understand, but in understanding he became too near being involved in the local reality. It was as if he need not be here at all, and certainly ought not to allow himself to be interested in a personal way with anything. He felt he might be trapped. But, with a sort of swimming sense of knowing that he could not say, he understood the words, which meant "What is your name? Mine is Carrica," and walked away as he answered, "My name is Jackson."

Then he felt himself vanishing, and the place he was in grew smaller and smaller around him and retreated from him, girl and pond and mist and hill, to be replaced by the dull fold of the staff room, where he was sitting in a chair by the window, Donald Jackson, with a memory of something like a dream growing fainter as he came more wholly into the staff room and saw the wall opposite, and Berry's hat on the floor and cloak on the chair.

Above the hat was a wooden plaque with gold lettering, a list of names, seen often enough and headed by more lettering that he had always known of, even before he came to the school. The Cecily Jackson Memorial Prize, it said, and under it the thirteen names of the winners of the prize. Cecily Jackson had been his sister, but that was all he knew, and by the time he had come into this world she had been no more in it.

A door opened in the building and a bell rang for the end of morning school. Donald sat up, because he had been slumped in the chair, but he did not get out of the room before Mr Dodwell, who taught English, came in.

"Hello Jackson, out of sorts?" he said. "It's usually one of the girls stretched out on three chairs with a hot-water-bottle. Are you all right now?"

"I'm fine," said Donald, "thank you sir. I was nearly sick, but I can eat my dinner now."

"Good," said Mr Dodwell. "Empty the hot-water-bottle and hang it in the staff lavatory before you go."

"Ha ha," said Donald, but not until he had gone out of the room and turned away.

II

MRS JACKSON CAME out of the staff entrance and caught up with Donald in the drive. They walked down it in the quiet throng of exodus. The wind, lessening now, was the noisiest thing, coming up behind people and giving them sudden pushes and dodging aside when it was leaned on. Mr Braxham sailed by with his arms wide under his cloak.

"It's a great help," he said, smiling at the ease with which he was moving along. Mrs Jackson smiled back, but only politely: the smile did not last beyond his passing or reach further than the outside of her lips.

"It'll be against him when he goes towards the vicarage," said Donald.

"It'll be against Daddy's car," said Mrs Jackson. Donald let the wind tune itself equally in either ear. He wanted to say something about the word 'Daddy', which he was no longer able to say easily because lately it had seemed so childish. But neither of them at home seemed to think anything was amiss with it, and all the embarrassment was his own. He wanted a quiet moment to mention it in, and this one, in the drive, was too noisy and too public.

"Once it could not get up the hill at all," said Mrs Jackson. "I had to wheel it in beside the Post Office and get a taxi."

In the next hour the wind ran out of breath, even up on the hill. The wetness left the sky, and the horizon of the sea became bright and distant. Donald sat at the table in his room and looked from the window, over the front hedge, over the road and the houses beyond, to the edge of the tide and the silken washed beach. Still in the gutter over the window the last of the fallen rain dripped, and now and then, in its last erratic puffs, the wind sighed in the roof over him. Outside the window the top of a small bush, looking in with its highest twigs and loaded with raindrops, refracted and focused its surroundings in gems. In the kitchen next to his room Donald heard tea being prepared. In the grass of the lawn a three-fingered glove danced alone, and lay still: a fallen and dried sycamore leaf, each lobe rolled, the palm curved.

In the road outside there was the approaching noise of the car, a tearing sound of the small engine working busily and the high whine of a fussy gear. The blue roof showed through the hedge, the engine spun against nothing for a moment, and then laboured to pull the car up the last slope out of the road. Donald watched it from a corner of his eye. It should have been coming up into the drive of the house, but it was making no progress. It was slipping sideways and scrabbling vainly with its tyres for a hold on the concrete. Donald jumped up from his chair, knocking a book to the floor, and hurried outside. He had forgotten what he had been asked to do: clear fallen leaves from the concrete.

By the time he got outside Mrs Jackson was already there with the brush, sweeping. The narrow blue car had stopped, and the engine was coughing to itself. Inside it Mr Jackson sat, waiting for the way to be cleared.

"Donald," said Mrs Jackson, letting him have the brush and this one word of reproof. Mr Jackson slid open the window of the car and looked at the drive, not at Donald, and waited.

The car was an invalid carriage, provided by the National Health Service. It was a single-seater, fitted with controls to suit Mr Jackson's abilities and disabilities. He could use his arms and hands, but his legs were hardly usable. The most he could do with them was use them as an extra prop, as a third crutch, so that he could stand for a time. There had been an accident that Donald had never had explained to him clearly, and the damage of the accident was paralysis and pain.

Donald shifted the leaves, put the brush against the wall, and pushed the car up the slope a little to start it on its journey. It went into its shelter with blue smoke pluming from it, and the engine died. Donald put the brush beside it and went indoors. Mr Jackson got out of the car in his own time and did not care to be watched as he struggled.

"You should have remembered, Donald," said Mrs Jackson, pouring water into the teapot. "What if he had had to come home before you and rest?"

"Some of the leaves came down during the day," said Donald.

"Not all of them," said Mrs Jackson. "It was mentioned this morning."

Mr Jackson wheeled himself in in the wheelchair and along to the bathroom. Mrs Jackson went along to help him, and Donald took the teapot to the table, feeling its senseless heat against his hands. Mrs Jackson pushed the wheelchair into the room again, and to the table, quietly. Once, Donald could remember, Mr Jackson had been prepared to race along the small passages of the house and make sudden swivelling turns and convincing racing car noises. Now he never did it.

He did not speak before tea, or during it, and after it he went to bed at once. Donald cleared away the tea things and began washing up. Mrs Jackson came through to help him after a time, and did the tidying of the kitchen that she said men never did properly. Donald went back to his homework and waited until half past seven. When that time came he went through to the living room and said, "It's Youth Guild night."

Mrs Jackson brought out a tenpenny piece and gave it to him. "Not feeling sick any more?" she asked.

"No, fine," said Donald. "Is he?"

"Daddy?" said Mrs Jackson. "No. It's just his back again. That's bad enough, of course, but something we're having to get used to, I'm afraid."

"The doctor would come if it was really bad," said Donald. "He always says he would, and give him an injection."

"We don't want to start on that before we have to," said Mrs Jackson. "We were meant to bear pain in this world, and what's sent to us we must submit to."

Before he left Donald had to submit to a scolding. He went to say goodnight, because Mr Jackson would be asleep before he came back from the Youth Guild. Mr Jackson was lying in bed, with the curtains closed to keep the light from his eyes. His hair was whiter than the pillow, and his face nearly as white and he held a hand to the side of his face. He blamed Donald for not sweeping the leaves away, not quite so much on account of the car but because Mrs Jackson had had to come out and do it. Then he warned him not to listen to the Church

22

religion of Mr Braxham, with whose opinions, personality and character he had no points of agreement, and regretted that Donald should ever have anything to do with him or the worldly Church of England, and hoped that he would never neglect the pure, regular, inspired faith of his own church, the Methodist one, with its particular calls to duty and service. Then Donald kissed him goodnight another thing he did not like to do any more, and say "Goodnight, Daddy," as if he were seven years old instead of nearly fifteen. Knocking fifteen, Berry said, in his more lively idiom.

Donald shut the house door on them and walked down the hill, with the wind not quite blowing but falling down the slope with him.

He was early still, and did not hurry. The Youth Guild was not only to do with Methodism. It was an inter-church group, and anyone could join. The Roman Catholics did not come, but in holiday times there had once been a Chinese family who were Buddhists, demonstrating the burning of joss sticks, nearly the same as incense. Tonight was Berry's turn to be mostly in charge, but he was nearly always late after visiting the nursing home. Everything happens on a Tuesday he would say; why didn't God invent the eight-day week and give us a chance to catch up?

Donald walked down by the sea towards the lower bridge over the river.

He was approaching the bridge when a gloom came over the sky, starting over the sea and spreading on to the land. The town became suddenly distinct under it, and then small and gemlike, as if it were reflected in a waterdrop on a bush outside a window. Then it went remote, and he was standing on a cart-track, not on a pavement, and his sleeve was no longer navy blue gaberdine but something like sacking.

He had come from the north. He had crossed a desolate place, and he was in a broken town, full of the ruins of abandonment and the misty, cold twilight. There were people about, but they were not noticing him, which was no surprise because he was unknown to them, a visitor, a passer-by, looking for somewhere to live. He stood and looked, and was hungry. This morning he had left the girl by the pond, and gone southwards again, only to meet once more the septic track over the land. He had turned away from it, and waited until the glow of the sun had begun to vanish before turning into the town again. He had seen people, but had not wanted to speak to them, because there was pain and difficulty in speaking to them. Now darkness was coming, and he had no shelter.

A man came walking down the hill past him, moving easily because he wore sandals. A question to him of one word, "Carrica?" brought only a push with an elbow and a look of scorn and affront. He stepped away from the man, and asked a boy the same thing. The boy wore only a short torn shirt, but he answered, and then led the way along a sort of street, or space among dwellings, into an alley, and pointed to a hut. The boy spoke, but translations of what he said was too disturbing a thing to attempt. When his mind began to manipulate the words a great unsteadiness came on him as if he did not know where he was and might be moved to some distant place if he went on thinking. Only the untranslateable word "Carrica", a name, did not threaten him. He said it to himself, and then said it aloud in what was now complete darkness. He did not say it loudly.

24

Somewhere among the houses, inside one of them, a man laughed, and a baby shouted. He heard all round him the noises of living, people settling for the night. Nowhere, though, was there a glimmer of light, nor even the usual accompaniment of evenings early dark, the smell of fires or cooking.

From a long way off, beyond the houses, beyond the limits of the town, there came a wailing, shimmering, bubbling cry, longer than a breath, it seemed, louder than a creature known to him. At that moment the noise held no fear for him, because he did not know what it was. But in the houses all round there was a silence.

He shouted out the girl's name. It was all he knew of this place, and he was hungry and shelterless. Even if she were married she could remember he had helped her.

There was silence after his shout. There was a merest scrape of a sound on the earth, and a feeling that behind him something was almost touching him, a sensation of the back of the leg. There was a wet sneeze at the back of his knee, and he knew it for a dog, and the feeling before that had been the same dog taking a long sniff at the same back of the knee, drawing a breath into its nostrils, and taking that air from his skin so that he felt his scent lifted off him. He put down his hand and touched the dog. It growled. He held it by the slack skin of its neck, and found it had a thong for a collar and held that instead, working his fingers round to the stone that hung on the thong and taking that in his palm.

Another hand was on the thong, seeking the same stone. Then it was on his wrist and he was being pulled through the darkness over blind ground, until he came stumbling and sprawling over the threshold of a building and into an even blinder darkness, thick and warm and full of the smell of people and dogs and babies and shelter.

His wrist was released, and he waited to see what happened. For a little while nothing happened. No one touched him, no one spoke. There was a scratching noise, as if a pebble were being dislodged from the floor. There was a fly of a spark in the blackness. There was more than that in a few beats of his heart. There was enough fire red in charcoal to show a man's face, and then there was heat against his own face, and he knew it was the same fire near him and that he was being looked at.

The fire was hidden away again. There was one small whisper in the darkness and that was the last sound. Silently the man approached, pushed him gently backwards until his knees met the sleeping shelf and he had to sit down. A contorted flake of bread was put in his hand, and he smelt the warm grease-crock nearby, and dipped the flake into it, edge by edge. That was supper, and he was sitting on a bed. He felt the man settle on the shelf and lie down, and climbed on for himself. He lay there in the darkness licking grease from his fingers and cheeks, and heard others shifting and breathing. On one side of this was the man, and on the other a younger man with hard shoulders. A dog slept at the back of the shelf and put out a sly invisible enquiring tongue to lick the grease from his cheek.

Sleep began to come to him, safe in this warm hut, and with sleep one of those wandering visions that visit the edge of sleep. He was being some other person, he found, in a crisp buzzing world of hard light and hard ground and hard people. Then, for a moment again he was Donald walking towards the bridge, and the boy who that morning, perhaps, had called

26

himself Jackson to a girl on a hillside. For a moment he could choose again which he would be. One is real, he said to himself. Donald is real. The other is a game of darkness, and I can be either and step from one to the other as I like. So he chose to stay on the sleeping shelf, without knowing how completely he became the person there. When he had come back to the dark he was thoroughly the boy from the north who was walking southwards to see what he found. He was no longer Donald, but only the son of Jack, the same character but a different person. He had had the choice of which to be, but it was one or the other. Neither person had the resources of the other, nor more than the smallest memory, or perhaps vestigial awareness, of the other's existence.

He settled to sleep. Jackson. The dog sighed in his ear. The house slept.

From the outside there came again the wailing cry, rising and falling in the dark, bubbling in itself and in its echo. Round him on the shelf he felt bodies become still and tense and stop breathing to listen. Now he felt the fear follow the cry, but fear shortened by custom, because when nothing happened immediately, while breath was held in expectation, the household began to fall asleep again.

Jackson slept. There was the digging of an elbow into him once, and he woke to find he had snored from being on his back. He turned on his side and curled up as well as he could between his two companions. The next time he woke was full of horror. It was a slow wakening, coming to consciousness uneasy and exploring the unease before moving or opening his eyes. Round him there was unnatural silence again, and the warm bodies either side of him were being held quiet. But there was a vibration in them, and in the whole shelf. And there was the smell, the stench, he had found on the hill, tightening his throat, making his cheeks run with sickening saliva, and his eyes scald with bitter waters. There was coldness in the house, a chill striking through the walls like a shadow, and the vibration went on.

From close at hand came the unknown sound again, bubling, gulping, howling. In the middle of it there was a human scream out in the night, and then half a scream and human silence, but the shrieking cadences continued from the thing that was not human, and the ground vibrated still.

The stench faded. It had come in from outside on the air, not in its own slimy substance. The vibration lessened, the howling stopped. Those in the house stayed wakeful and waiting, until there was a relaxing of tension by the man. Then there was a sudden flurry of movement from the other sleeping shelf, and the sleepers there had crossed the hut and come to share with the menfolk. He knew it was Carrica who came in beside him because there was still on her shift the faded smell of the tract on the hill where he had found her that morning.

She was not alone. There was a desperate quiet scramble across the shelf for room, and the party ended by being stacked like logs, a lower layer of larger people, and an upper layer of small ones lying in the valleys between the larger ones. Jackson found, in front of him, the man whose face he had seen, and between them and on top someone with long hair, not very heavy. Behind him was Carrica or some other girl, because he could feel the shape of her bosom on his back by his shoulder-blades when he breathed in.

Then all sensation fell away, not into sleep, but into being

Donald, who found himself walking still down to the bridge with an impression of something apprehended but not seen now vanishing. It was as if a television screen, displaying sensation, not mere sight, were shrinking to nothing, taking everything with it except the awareness that there had been something.

That passed. Donald crossed the bridge and walked to the Parish Room. He was still early, so he went in and arranged the chairs. Mr Braxham liked informality, so he put them in a loose circle. They had been put by the caretaker in rows. Donald wondered why it was easier to think ahead for Berry, and do what he liked, but not quite so easy at home, where his duty much more lay.

Nessing was next to come, and after him the two spotty Wilbert girls, eating sweets and arranging themselves stylishly in chairs at the point where the circle ran into the wall and could not be more than one row deep. They set themselves out on display always, but they were only playing, because they were interested in sweets and comics but not in boys. One of them was rather pretty, Donald thought, in spite of spots. She was the unintelligent one in the remedial class. The other one was in a parallel form to Donald. Nessing went to talk to her, or at least make coarse comments loudly. Donald stood by the door. He felt it was his duty not to be chatting to Jacqueline Wilbert when Berry came in.

When he did come in, five minutes late, and Donald had been by the door for more than ten minutes, he had his left arm round the shoulders of Jack Copsey, and his right arm round the shoulders of Lanky Errington, and swept through the double doors with them, passing Donald in mid-sentence unacknowledged, before releasing Copsey and Errington, turning about with a swirl of the cloak and giving Donald a not very special smile. Then he sat down next to Jacqueline Wilbert, to be impartial, and began the Guild meeting.

III

It was curious, Donald thought towards the end of the Guild meeting, how a dogmatic, schematic religion like the Church of England with its bishops (which is what Mr Jackson said about it) should have so many points where things were not clear; while an inspirational sect like Methodism, though it had its schemes, and though it relied on waiting for the word of God to strike through its members and fire them into action, had fewer points of doubt and argument. The meeting had been what Berry called an open-ended argument, so open-ended that anything put into it fell right through without affecting what was being talked about. Donald thought that his own religious quality and his ability to receive inspiration must be minimal. Then the meeting finished, and the girls said "Good night, Mr Braxham", because it was understood that they did not call him Berry, and went out, but most of the boys stayed. Then there were two rough, pushing games of table tennis, and it was time to put out the lights and leave.

"It's early still," said Berry, closing the door on the warm dusty air in the parish hall, where all the talk and the shouting had wilted into silence. "Who's coming home with me?"

Donald and Nessing and two other boys thought it was too soon to go to their own homes. Donald would quite have liked to fall in by chance with Jacqueline Wilbert and her pretty smile, and walk along with her, even if she rarely spoke, and if she did it was to say something that had been going round in her mind and had nothing to do with what had been said to her that day. Nessing took Berry's cloak and wore it. Donald took his hat and felt it hard and loose on his head. It belonged more to Berry's curls.

"Do you," said Nessing, noticing how the hat did not fit so snugly on Donald, "curl your hair, Berry?"

"I straighten it," said Berry. "But that's vanity too. I sleep in uncurl papers, some plastic unrollers. You should see me scrubbing the front door step of a morning, dear, with me shawl over me head, it would make you weep to see the drudgery we poor girls put up with, five o'clock sharp, or we lose our places. Mind you I quite enjoy putting that white line round it when I've finished."

Berry was talking nonsense, of course, but even that brought pity to Donald's heart.

"I once went along a whole street in Sheffield," said Nessing, "and they all had white lines on the step, and I had my new sneakers on with those dug-out soles and heels, and I left a black print on each step."

"You don't get good marks," said Berry, "for inciting other people to show Christian forbearance towards you."

"I'm all right now," said Nessing. "I confessed, didn't I? I gave them marks. Perhaps I get marks for being forgiven."

"Donald doesn't agree," said Berry. "And we've had enough argument for one night. Let's go and see what's cooking at home."

32

Berry had married the daughter of a bishop. It was said that he had done so to help his career by knowing the right people. They had two adopted children, a boy and a girl. Berry called them both Toby and said he had chosen them for the colour of their eyes, because brown eyes were best and hadn't looked any further because he didn't care. They were both very young and called him Belly. Nessing's eyes were green, Donald's were blue or grey, one of the other boys had hazel eyes, and the other very dark blue.

Berry was putting together an elaborate plastic model of a sailing ship for the children, not very handily. The glue had smudged it and softened the surfaces. Nessing, helplessly unable to stop himself destroying things, opened a little pot of plastic paint and dipped the paint brushes in it, and left them to dry solid. Berry glued on a section of rail quarter of an inch out of line and held it with a cemented thumb. Mrs Braxham made lumpy coffee in the kitchen and the diapered children crawled dustily under the hearth rug.

When they went Berry came to the gate with them and held Donald back for a little while with a hand on the back of his neck. They leaned on the gate.

"Have you recovered now?" he said. "You look all right, but you seem a bit quiet tonight. Anything on your mind?"

"No," said Donald. "Nothing confessable."

"Everything's confessable," said Berry.

"I mean there's nothing on my conscience except forgetting things at home," said Donald.

"Oh, good," said Berry. Donald thought he was a little disappointed and would have liked to hear of a sin or two. "How are they at home?"

"Daddy has his pain tonight," said Donald.

"That's a worry," said Berry. "Isn't it?"

"Yes," said Donald, but he said no more than that, because the pain was not quite the worry. What he noticed most about the pain Mr Jackson had to bear was his own inability to appreciate and understand it. It meant to him a white-faced man of uncertain temper and dour disposition, and the necessity of keeping quieter than usual, and these did not occur to him as matters for confession, though perhaps they were.

"I'll come up," said Berry. "Tomorrow. I don't see enough of your family, not as much as I should like. I feel they don't appreciate you enough as a person, because of their very real difficulties. But I mustn't keep you now, unless there is anything and you want to stay."

"Only one thing," said Donald, opening the gate. "I think Nessing was playing with your paint and brushes and didn't clean the brushes and that stuff dries hard."

"Oh, ha," said Berry, "then I'd better go in." He slapped the top of the gate twice as a farewell, thinking Donald's hand was there, and walked back to his open front door. Donald walked home under starlight and lamplight alternately, wondering how he could have said he wanted to stay longer in the dirty untidy friendly vicarage, talking about nothing, being part of the sporadic spontaneity of a normal household. Even Nessing had a normal household, with two dogs, a little sister who was even more destructive than he was (she would tear up the clothes she was sitting in if things went against her) and a father who was quite amiable and who became drunk about three times a year and leaned on shop windows until they fell in. He would have to stay in bed the next day, feeling quite ill

34

and often bleeding, but it was in order for him to be laughed at for his pain, if not at the time, then a day or two later.

When Donald came home Mrs Jackson was marking books. She put her finger against her lips to keep him from talking, then laid the book aside that she was working on, and walked through to the bedroom. He heard her speak, and move Mr Jackson a little on the mattress. She came out again and closed the doors behind her.

"He isn't sleeping," she said. "You could do to go to bed early as well, after this morning. Was it a long Guild meeting?"

"We went on to Berry—Mr Braxham's afterwards," said Donald. "He said he might come up tomorrow."

"Mmn," said Mrs Jackson, drawing a line through a word in one of the books and writing the correct one in small and red above it.

"He doesn't know you enough," said Donald. "He only knows me."

"What?" said Mrs Jackson. "I must finish these, Jackson, so don't chatter. If you want anything will you get it for yourself? I've got quite a lot to do."

"I'll go to bed," said Donald.

"Quietly," said Mrs Jackson. "Use the outside lavatory."

When he was in his own room, with the door closed to keep his own noise in and the house noises out, Donald finished the home-work that was on the table, and put all the books away. He heard Mr Jackson call out and Mrs Jackson put down her books and go to him. He sat on his bed and waited for that season of activity to stop, wanting to pierce the secret of what was happening, but not wanting to be involved. Mrs Jackson went back to her books in a little while. Donald got out his Bible and read the appointed passage, then turned to the inside of the back cover. Here there was kept a small photograph of a girl.

He had assumed, once, that it was his sister's photograph, but he had not asked because she was not mentioned very often, and the most references to her came from people outside, and the board in the staff room at school, and another at the chapel: "In whose memory this chapel was restored and modernised" and a date of a dozen years ago. It might be Cecily and it might not. Sometimes he wanted it to be and sometimes he wanted it to be a stranger; a stranger who was not unknown, not strange; one who belonged to him alone out of the whole circle of being, to whom he could be himself without modification. With no one else, not even with Berry, could he be himself, untouched by all his background. He looked at the picture for a little while, until by being looked at hard it became only shadow and shadow and less and less real. He put it back in the Bible and put the Bible away, switched off the light and got into bed.

It was a long night. He woke twice, the first time clear into the sounds of moving in the other bedroom, and voices hushed. The second time he seemed to be waking not alone but huddled with others, close against him behind and before, but he struggled through into actuality, and saw the light round the door and heard again the low voices he had often heard before, and lay awake hearing and not wanting to listen, and slept again.

He woke again when Mrs Jackson touched his shoulder and told him to dress quietly because Daddy was sleeping at last.

"You should get a doctor," said Donald, with his first breath, but Mrs Jackson had gone then, leaving him in the grey-green morning light. He sat up and held his feet, put his cheeks against his knees and closed his eyes.

It was lighter with his eyes shut. There was a doorway with a nearly sunny mist beyond it, and there were people talking. He opened his eyes again, and it was his dark bedroom. He closed his eyes again, and was dragged away into that other place.

The hut door was open. He was sitting on the sleeping shelf, with his feet on the floor. He was holding a bowl of thin milky stuff and drinking it. It was a warm drink. The doorway darkened, and in came the man of the house. On the other bench was Carrica and some small children. There was talking. The little children were jumping up and down, now sitting, now standing, now kneeling, and asking "Who was it? How many was it? Can we go and see?"

"Keep out of the trail; we don't want that tramped in here," said the man. "And be sharp, we want you in the field. Carrica, you take Jackson and show him."

He remembered that he had said he was Jackson when they woke up.

"Jackson belongs to me," said Carrica. "You others keep off."

"To me, to me, to me, to me as well," the little ones shouted.

"Be quiet, all of you," said the woman of the house, looking up red-faced from the fire-pot. "Jackson brought you from danger, Carrica. Thank him, and then thank God, and ask for Jackson to be delivered from the dangers we have been kept from for so long."

"And grant that he may be fortified against all assaults of evil," said Carrica. "Thank you, Jackson, for saving me."

Jackson wanted to ask what he had saved her from, because no one had told him yet. No one told him now. He thought they might be Christians. He had met Christians before, and it did not seem to matter; all had to work in fields and houses, all eat and drink.

Carrica came across and put his bowl on the floor, and the dog nosed it and overturned it. "We'll go and see," she said. "Then we'll go to the county field."

They went out of the hut into the restricted daylight under the misty sky.

"It's cold," he said.

"It's a cold trouble," said Carrica. "It's warmer in the fields."

The little children had come out of the hut with them. Inside it they had been eager to come out, but now they were out they stood against Carrica and Jackson and did not run about or shout.

"I suppose you will go away soon, when you see what sort of place it is and what there is here," said Carrica.

"I don't know what *is* here," said Jackson.

"Come and see," said Carrica. "What it was last night."

"What I heard, and smelt?" said Jackson.

"That," said Carrica. "It was over here."

They went down between the huts to the edge of the river. Down by the bank more people stood, quiet and watching, along a line in the ground beyond which no one went. From a distance there seemed no reason for staying to one side of an unmarked boundary, but as Jackson and the girl came nearer they smelt the smell that had come in the night and on the hill the previous day. In the ground in the middle of the town was the same compressed stinking track, coming up out of the river. The track had not gone far into the town. It went to a crushed hut, a better hut than some, with stone walls, but the walls were burst apart, and the woodwork was splintered and spread. Men were standing carefully on the fallen stones and looking into the shell of the building. They were standing and moving carefully because on the stones and all round was the cold, foul, sickening jelly that covered the track.

"They have all gone," said a man, coming down from the wall. "My sister and her husband and both children and the dog."

Further away some boys were doing a sort of fishing with long sticks for something in the track, and by the edge of the river a man was engaged in the same thing. They were all trying to bring in some bundles of stuff, greyish bundles about a foot across and the shape of a ball. The bundle in the water of the river was floating. The bundles in the track were light too, and the sticks brought them closer to the side. The boys and the man waited for each other to have the bundles safe, and then they worked the ends of the sticks into them, without touching with their hands, and carried them back and laid them down again.

"What is it?" said Jackson. "What are those?"

"They are what it leaves," said Carrica. "It is their clothes and their hair. When it has taken them it leaves those, and that is all we have to bury."

Jackson looked closer, and saw that it was so. The bundles were rags not long torn, mingled with long hair. Rags and hair alike were bleached greyish white, and the smell was strong on them.

"What is it?" said Jackson, although he thought he knew now, that he had heard of the thing that behaved as this unknown thing behaved.

"It is the worm," said Carrica. "It is a huge worm, that came from the sea up the river and lives up the valley, and lives on people from the town."

"A worm, a serpent, a monster," said Jackson.

"All those," said Carrica. "It is all those. And it went past yesterday when I was coming from the county field, and it came in the night and took away these people," and she indicated the four bundles, and then a fifth small handful that a boy brought, that had been the dog. In that bundle the curved dog's teeth showed, clean and long.

"So you will go," said Carrica. "There are too many of us to go, so we must stay."

"Yes," said Jackson, "I shall go."

The girl looked at him, and he looked back. She swirled away into the distance, shrinking out of his recognition, with the five bundles beside her and the crowd beyond them. Donald opened his eyes, which were against his knees now, wondered at the brightness, opened himself up and got out of bed.

During breakfast Mr Jackson woke again and wanted to get up himself and go to work. Not going to work made him feel useless and burdensome. He and Mrs Jackson had a long talk about it, that was not over when Donald was ready to leave for school and Mrs Jackson came back to talk to him.

"I shan't be in today," she said. "You'll have guessed. Will you give this note to the headmaster, and these corrected books in to Form IIIa. Better give them to Mr Dodwell, he's their master, and this note so that he can set them some work to do."

"Sure," said Donald. "Shall I come back for dinner? Would it be useful?"

"No, don't worry," said Mrs Jackson. "Stay at school, and then I can get some sleep whenever I like. I hope Mr Braxham doesn't come."

"I'll run round and tell him," said Donald.

"Tell him we had a bad night," said Mrs Jackson. "That's all."

Berry was in his kitchen, washing up. His wife was upstairs with the children. Beside the sink, on the draining board, were the two brushes Nessing had dipped, standing in a jam jar of water, pathetic, spoilt.

"Message from Mum," said Donald, when Berry had finished his invitation to enter and offers of breakfast and matins. "She says please don't come today because they've been awake all night and they want to get to sleep today if they can."

"Oh yes, quite understood, don't worry about it," said Berry. "Another time will be better, eh?"

"I think so," said Donald. "Those paint brushes won't be any good."

"None at all," said Berry. "Nessing's a bastard, tell him from me."

IV

DONALD'S WALK HOME after school counterpointed his walk home the night before from Berry's, where he had stepped from light to light of the streetlamps, separate pools lying apart, and gone through starlight between. The following frost had scorched off hung leaves from the trees and let them fall to the still ground below. Now there were, in the afternoon daylight and sunshine, circles of faded carpet along the streets, like the glow of lamps but in different, unrelated places, and between these circles with their unsewn edges lay the starlit desert of cloudless pavement.

Donald walked through these open-plan unwalled rooms without much noticing them. A thick green was an ash tree, and a busy sandy pattern a sycamore, and a rich radiant pattern from a half-clear tree was a copper beech, reflecting red light from the ground to the palm of an outheld hand, and light through the leafed branches shining positively red on the back of it, as if it went through a boneless limb.

Mrs Jackson was dealing with leaves too, sweeping the drive of the bungalow and gathering the sweeping into heaps and the heaps into barrowloads.

"I'll do that," said Donald, taking the brush from her.

"No," said Mrs Jackson, "I'm doing it to get a little air and exercise while Daddy's asleep."

"I thought he must be going out, if you're sweeping the drive," said Donald.

"He's still in bed," said Mrs Jackson. "And I expect another wakeful night."

"You should get the doctor," said Donald. "And that injection."

"We've been through this before," said Mrs Jackson. "These attacks of pain, and you wanting the doctor each time."

"I would want him if they were my attacks," said Donald.

"You haven't yet a background of belief and a habit of trust in the Lord," said Mrs Jackson. "Daddy knows that what he has to bear is not more than he *can* bear."

"It's more than *I* can bear," said Donald.

"I know what you mean," said Mrs Jackson. "Necessary fortitude in the sufferings of others can be acquired, Donald, but it is one of the more difficult gifts. It's one that doctors don't have, with all their remedies that they can pump in to bring you back to normal, or what they call normal. But God's intention is not always normality, is it?"

"We have different normals," said Donald.

"And different strengths and weaknesses," said Mrs Jackson. "You know it would be no use me trying to teach music or physical education or history."

"I'll go and do my homework," said Donald.

Mr Jackson stayed asleep through tea and for an hour afterwards. When he woke and had had a cup of tea himself he sent for Donald. Donald finished a maths problem he was doing and went through to the bedroom. Mr Jackson had been looking through the window at the western landward sky, and he looked blindly at Donald when he came in because Donald was hidden by darkness. Donald saw the searching eyes and wondered what had happened, but it was not explained to him. He thought that Mr Jackson must have become partly blind during this attack of pain. When Donald spoke Mr Jackson located his voice and looked towards that, found a clearing in the darkness, and Donald in it, and was able to look at him.

"What are you going to be?" he said.

"I don't know," said Donald. "We don't have to decide until the summer term."

"That's when you have to say what you've already decided," said Mr Jackson. "What are you doing about it?"

"I'll see what I'm good at," said Donald. "That's the way we have to do it."

"Maybe," said Mr Jackson. "I don't think that's very positive. You should know by now, Donald. If you had listened to the voices of wisdom, you would know how you are to serve the Kingdom of Heaven, and what road you should take towards it, and everything you need will be added to you. What I need has been added to me, Donald." Then Mr Jackson slipped away from talking to Donald and started to preach as if he were in the chapel. Donald sat and waited through it, because he knew that the sermon had to come to its own end and would not stop before then. In chapel he could bear such talking, about personal failure to be as great as God intended because of flawing the perfect character that was given to you to start with. Chapel preachings were bearable, because it was possible to see other people not quite attending all the time, and because there was shelter in being in the crowd. But preaching from the authority of Mr Jackson direct to himself, about

44

matters of failure that could only be his own shortcomings and weaknesses was different in the way it was heard, though just the same in the way it was said. And on this occasion there was something else added to the discourse, a note that was more than anxiety. Mr Jackson's voice grew higher in pitch and a sort of tense excitement took over, and the talk went away from Donald towards the sky again. Donald was alarmed in a while, because he was forgotten, he knew, and Mr Jackson's eyes were staring towards nothing, and a sickly red was in his cheeks and forehead and he was praying fast and unintelligibly, and, Donald thought, blasphemously, using the words of Christ in the garden of Gethsemane, asking for the cup to be taken from him.

"My father has gone mad," said Donald to himself, words of logic and not feeling. He shifted in his chair, but Mr Jackson did not notice, but continued to address the sky. The fast speech had left bubbles of spit in the corners of his mouth. Donald stood up, and his heart noticed and burst into loud unaccustomed rhythm, and cold sweat ran down his ribs from his armpits and his breath slammed back and forth across his chest. Mr Jackson took no notice when Donald walked softly across the floor and out of the room. He went on talking. Outside, in the passage, Donald stopped to breathe quietly. There was pain in his back, and a reducing tingle in all his limbs and a curling in his belly. He felt as he had felt when he stepped over the cliff once, and while he had had time to grab the edge he had had time as well to see where he might have gone, down the muddy face among the poppies and into the sea. But this time he had not thumped himself as well. He went into the kitchen, and spoke, still short of breath.

45

"He's strange," he said. "Go through."

Mrs Jackson went through without a word. Donald stood where he was for a time, then went to his own room, and wondered what was now going on at Mr Jackson's bed. There was talking still, and then there was quieter talking, and then there was quiet. On his table the maths book lay untended. Outside the night fell blue.

Mrs Jackson came in after a time and smiled to him. "He was a little excited and hysterical," she said. "I think he's a little feverish. I expect the same infection brought the pain on last night. However, he's settled for the night now."

Donald wept when she had gone, with guilt for suspecting true madness in the house, and with misery at not being able to distinguish the words and intentions of God from all the ordinary matters that came to his attention all day and in dreams all night (like Samuel). Then he went to bed himself.

The night was broken for him, the first time by mere movement in the other room, and the second time when his own door was opened and Mrs Jackson switched on the light. "Will you get up?" she said, and went back again to the other room. Donald got dressed, and then did not know what to do but wait. From the other room there came sighing groans and unformed words. He dared not go to that door, but stood in his own room. Mrs Jackson came out pretty soon. "Are you awake?" she said. Donald said he was. "Go down to the call box and telephone the doctor," she said. "Here's the money, and I've written the number on this paper." Donald saw the number, and the name in her small red writing, and tucked the paper into his pocket. "Ask the doctor to come, please, because I don't know what's wrong. Go on, quickly."

The time was twenty-five past two by the kitchen clock. In the streets outside the lamplight lay inelastic and hard on the road and houses, cut and unforgiving where walls rose in its path and forced it to leap shadows like gulfs. It lay spread and exact and unheeding, not caring about humans but existing alone in its own right.

Donald stood in the cold telephone box, a cold room in a cold world, lit by a yellow lamp in the roof and the white lamps of the street. He spread the paper on the shelf, got out the coin Mrs Jackson had given him, and dialled. The telephone rang in some far room. Then it was picked up and answered. Donald dropped the money into the slot, and the coin fell straight through. He tried again, and the coin evaded the grip of the machine three times. Donald explained what was happening, but the doctor at the other end could not hear him at all. Then the doctor put his telephone back, and there was only the dialling tone again.

Donald dialled once more, but the line was engaged, twice. He was just opening the directory to find the doctor's address, to see whether it was near enough to run straight there when a a car stopped outside and a policeman got out and came to the box and pulled the door open.

"Who are you ringing, son?" he said.

"Dr Riley," said Donald. "But it's a dud coin, I think, and I haven't got another, so can you change it."

"Jump in the car," said the policeman. "We'll take you round there. He told us someone was ringing him, so we thought we'd look, in case it was someone up to their tricks."

"No, not that," said Donald. He came out of the box and the policeman looked in.

47

"Your money," he said, picking the coin from the shelf. He picked up the note with the doctor's name and number on it. He looked at the coin, and said it seemed to be a good one, it was the thin ones that slipped through. He dropped it into the slot and it stayed in. He got it out again by pressing a button. "No trouble," he said. Donald watched him, and thought he must have put the coin in the slot to the right, for a larger piece of money, but it was not worth saying anything. He took the coin and the note from the policeman and walked out to the car.

The doctor lived not far away. There was a light on downstairs, and the doctor was in his dressing-gown and came to the door. Donald got out, with the policeman, feeling that he had come a long midnight journey and that this ought to be the end of it.

"I know this boy," said Dr Riley, sharply, so that Donald felt like abandoning his message and running straight back home.

"Tell him your message, son," said the policeman.

"Come inside, boy," said Dr Riley, standing back from the door and letting only Donald in. The policeman stood outside.

Donald gave the message. Dr Riley nodded, opened the door and spoke to the policeman. "No nonsense there," he said. "Just never learned to use the telephone, that's all. Oh, a bungalow up on Hales Hill. Will you? Good." Then he turned to Donald. "They'll run you back," he said. "I'll be along in a few minutes, tell your mother. Go on, out you go."

So Donald went out again, and the policeman led him by the elbow to the car, which turned about, and skated from pool to pool of light and up the hill and dropped him at his door. Before he had got up the drive the car had turned again and gone down, leaving on the air a voice from its radio.

Mrs Jackson came to the door when she heard the car, and watched it go while she tried to work out what was happening.

"The doctor's coming," said Donald, giving back the coin and the slip of paper.

"Go back to bed, Donald," said Mrs Jackson. Donald went through to his room, undressed and got into bed. From the other room came the regular recurrent groaning that had been there before he went out into the dark.

He was conscious of movement and speaking, but the noises went over into sleep. It was daylight when he blinked into being again, and the kettle had whistled for boiling and stopped at once. He was already getting up when Mrs Jackson opened his door. There was quiet from the other room.

They spoke quietly in the kitchen while he ate breakfast.

"It was the only thing to do," said Mrs Jackson. "He's resting better for it now; asleep in fact. The doctor's coming again before surgery starts."

"Surgery?" said Donald, thinking of scalpels in the house and the red of waste blood.

"Before patients come to visit him," said Mrs Jackson. "I didn't mean anything else."

Donald saw the car in the town on his way to school. Dr Riley, dressed now for the day, gave him a nod and drove on up Hales Hill. Donald looked at the back of the car, and turned away.

He came back home from school in the afternoon with a feeling that there would be calm, if not happiness, at home, and a sense of sated tiredness riding his shoulders. He unlocked the door and came in, and there was quiet indeed, and he wondered why the fire had gone out. He went to his room and put his books on the table, and sat down to look at them.

There was too much quietness, he thought, and uneasily he went back into the kitchen. Not only was the fire out, but he saw his breakfast dishes still on the table, and the bread in its crumbs on the board. The house sat cold and threatening, oppressive and sinister. He went back towards his room, and let his eyes look at the other room.

In the doorway was the end of a sheet, drawn to a crumpled point. He went to the door and looked in. The room was empty of people. The bed had been left unmade, and more than unmade. The covers had been dragged back and spread on the floor, and all was cold. He went out of the room, and out of the house. The car was still in its place. The milk stood by the doorstep. He took it in and put it away, and wondered what had happened. The front door swung to behind him and latched itself, closing the house on him once more. He was alone in it.

There was a tapping at the door. He went to it, and there was Mrs Ross from next door.

"Donald," she said, "your Mum had to go with him." Then, seeing that he did not understand she wrapped her fingers in her apron and explained more clearly that Mr Jackson had been taken away to the hospital early in the morning. "I thought you would know," she said.

"No," said Donald. "What was it for?"

"Observation," said Mrs Ross. "They do that first. Would you like to come in and get your tea with us?"

"I'll go down in the town," said Donald. "When will she be back?"

"She couldn't say," said Mrs Ross. "She just asked me to look out for you, but I didn't see you until you came for the milk, and I thought how calmly he's taking it. Now, if you do want anything then we're there, me and Mr Ross."

"Well, thank you," said Donald. She went away. Donald closed the door. He thought he might go to bed at once, or light the fire and sit by it, but the house was too full of silence for that, and he did what he had said to Mrs Ross. He gathered up his books again and walked down Hales Hill and through the town to Berry's vicarage.

Berry was making large clumsy toast, and his wife was letting baked beans scorch in the pan and making tea from water that had gone off the boil.

"We're just feasting," said Berry, who was at the kitchen door when Donald came, scraping black from the toast. "It's burnt offerings again today, if you want any."

"There's no one at home," said Donald. "They've taken Daddy to hospital, and I think Mum's there with him."

"Oh, I'm sorry," said Berry. "Come straight in and sit down. You look as if you're at the end of your tether."

Donald was rather at the end of his tether: he had eaten out all the circle of life round himself. But the baked beans and jam and tea with floating leaves revived him. At the end of the meal he still felt tired, but comforted. "I've just remembered," he said, "Mum won't know where I am if she's come home."

"If we pinned a message to one of those Tobies," said Berry, "and set it crawling in the direction of your house, it would get there in the end. They only crawl in straight lines, you know."

"She won't worry yet," said Donald.

"That's all right," said Berry. "We'll sit here and talk jolly stuff for a bit, and then I have to go out and I'll put a message in as I go by, and that's everybody notified."

They went into the study and played with the Tobies for a time, and talked about the sea. Berry thought it would be a good idea to have a troop of Sea Scouts, because the sea was there ready to be used, just as made even before the first day. "Though they might be sick," said Berry, "throw up and give up. Anyway, I've only just thought of it, and I'm going so soon. That reminds me, I have to go out. You settle here, Donald, as long as you like. Look after the Tobies, and if you want anything, sing out, and the handmaid will get it for you, no doubt. I've never tried it myself, so I can't guarantee it. I'll be about forty minutes. If anyone comes wanting to be married or converted or exorcised, just do your best." He touched Donald's head, dumped a Toby on him, and went out. The Toby crawled off Donald's lap and went smudging about the floor. The other one woke from a philosophical trance and laughed at him.

Donald brought out a history text book and opened it. Then it had gone from his hand, and he was no longer Donald in the vicarage but Jackson in the dark town, standing with Carrica by the ruins of a hut, and close by five bundles of rejected matter that had once been living people.

"Here he comes," said Carrica. "The new lord."

A horseman was coming. The horse smelt the smell of the worm and began to refuse to come closer. The rider fought with it and forced it on, and it came reluctantly and stood by the ruins.

"What lord is it?" asked Jackson.

"The newest," said Carrica. "They are all killed, or they do not fight, and they send another."

"I don't know what happens here," said Jackson.

"We are not allowed to leave the town," said Carrica. "Instead the worm kills us. The lord is supposed to protect us and to kill the worm, but it will not be killed, it kills them instead. So they send us another lord. We do not always know their names. This one has only just come."

"What is he called?" said Jackson. He had met lords as he travelled. Some had given him shelter, some had run him from their lands, and some had fined him for wandering and put him to work until he had paid off the fine in work.

"Breakbone," said Carrica. "Lord Breakbone he is called here, but I do not know his real name, lords do not use their real names."

The lord looked at the scene. No one spoke. He handed his spear to a man nearby and got off the horse, then exchanged the spear for the reins. He did not climb on the ruins. He touched the bundles of rags with the spear, tearing one of them open. The lord wore a red tunic, and inside the bundle he tore there was red cloth, spotted and faded, but red.

"I shall need another boy," he said, turning and looking about. "What about you?" he said, touching a boy on the shoulder with the butt of the spear.

The boy moved away a pace, but the spear butt came with him and tapped him hard on the shoulder where he had only been touched before. A woman came out of the crowd. "Lord," she said, "this is the only man of the house, and we have paid our dues, all except the road service, and that has not been levied yet."

53

"You are released," said the lord. "I will find another for the honour." He looked about him and saw Jackson.

"It is a good service," said Carrica. "Until the worm gets you."

"Come here, boy," said the lord. "Why should *you* not serve?"

"I am not a citizen," said Jackson.

"Nor am I," said the lord. "Come with me." He turned and mounted the horse, threw the spear upright to Jackson, took up his reins, and turned the horse away from the riverside. Jackson caught the spear. Carrica put her hand on his for a moment, and stepped away. Jackson walked after the horse.

"Run," said a man he passed. "Run after the lord."

Jackson ran. The lord saw him from the corner of his eye and motioned him to run alongside. They went, man, horse and boy, up from the hovels and huts of the riverside to the stone buildings on the side of the hill, and up again, when they were in the narrow streets, to the highest building castled round its courtyard, and in through the gate. Here the lord dismounted, waited for Jackson to take the reins, saying "Be ready, boy, be ready," and went into the building. Jackson stood there with the reins in his hand, until there was a shout from an archway and he was told to bring that horse in sharply, lad. He walked towards the archway, and the horse, after a little resistance, came with him, putting its head down to nibble his shoulder. Then the darkness of the arch ahead swung away, and he was sitting in an easy chair in the vicarage and the Toby was still laughing at him and the history book was still in his hand.

V

DONALD HAD NEVER been in the empty vicarage before—Mrs Braxham and the two Tobies did not count as part of Berry at all—and in some ways he might just as well have been at home in the empty rooms there. But here there was the expectation of seeing Berry as soon as he came back. There was no way of telling when Mrs Jackson would come in, and no convenient way for her to send him a message either. He settled to his history book again, and decided that the two Tobies were a convenient sort of company, able to move about but not to talk, to be more attractive than animals and less demanding. All the same they did not disregard him, but kept coming near and touching him, hoisting themselves up to a standing position by his knee, and then falling down, shaking the floor gently. Mrs Braxham sang to herself in the kitchen, washing up slowly.

A visitor came to the kitchen door. Mrs Braxham opened it and spoke to someone outside. Donald heard Mrs Jackson's voice, and got up at once. He hoped she would come in, and he could hear her being asked. He wanted her and Berry to be better friends. But she did not come in. Donald gathered up his books and his coat and stepped over several Tobies, three he thought, but perhaps he had to step over one of them twice, or had started counting at two. He went through to the kitchen.

Mrs Jackson was standing in the garden, looking in. Donald went out to her, and then turned to thank Mrs Braxham, who said Berry would be sorry he had gone.

Mrs Jackson did not speak as they went down the path, and Donald did not ask her anything. He was clasping his books and fastening his coat. They walked slowly into the road in a sweet autumn twilight, luminous everywhere, with the street lamps concentrated drops of the bright sky above, not yet casting their own glare.

Still Mrs Jackson did not speak. She was tired, and her shoulders were rounded with fatigue. Dark against the end of the street came the cloaked figure of Berry, approaching and smiling, walking quicker when they saw him.

"Hello," he said. "How goes it, Mrs Jackson?"

"He's resting very quietly, Mr Braxham," said Mrs Jackson. "He has some inflammation of the lung, and he is only in hospital because of the difficulties of home nursing."

"Yes, indeed," said Mr Braxham. "I need hardly say that anything I can do will naturally be a pleasure to me, any hospitality for you or Donald, any errands which we or the Scouts can carry out, any spiritual matters. . . ."

"Thank you for giving Donald his tea," said Mrs Jackson, across the end of Berry's speech. "We mustn't trouble you any further tonight."

"You will want to be home," said Berry, meaninglessly. "Come by any time, Donald; open house, you know."

"And jolly talk," said Donald.

"And jolly talk," said Berry. He raised his hat and flowed off down the street.

At home the grate was still empty. Donald brought in sticks

and lit the fire, tidied the breakfast things away, and put on the kettle.

"I wish you had done that when you came back before," said Mrs Jackson. "Mrs Ross would have given you tea, and I would have had no need to trail down to the vicarage for you. This is your home, in every way. But I'm tired and impatient and unreasonable, so put the kettle on (Donald had already done that and it was heating from within) and make some tea."

Mrs Jackson went through to the bedroom. Donald heard her making the bed, after she had hung up her coat. He made the tea, and then looked blankly at the larder, not knowing what to do next, but knowing she would want something to eat. There was again that slight tap at the door, and it was Mrs Ross.

"I saw your lights go on," she said. "Though I smelt the fire being lit first, and I thought I'd come over with this hot pie, I made extra thinking you would come in. How is he, your father? I'll just put it in the oven, clap cold though it is, but it'll soon draw round."

"His lung is inflamed," said Donald. "He's there because Mum can't nurse him here."

"No, there would be problems," said Mrs Ross. "And he has so much to put up with when he had no need, I mean, look what he did with all that compensation, not that it's any of my business, but (and she hurried what she was saying because Mrs Jackson was coming along the passage) I would have done things differently. Mrs Jackson, you look beat, if you don't mind me saying so."

"In some ways I'm glad to be home," said Mrs Jackson, "where I know everybody and everything. Though I know that hospital too well from last time, but of course it was a different part today, but it's the same journey."

"And I used to look after Donald then," said Mrs Ross. "He was just a tiny mite, so small."

Donald, pretty big now, he thought, poured tea for all three of them, and sat down at the far side of the fireplace to drink his. Mrs Jackson touched the oven and looked inside it, and said she would drink tea first and then see whether she could manage to eat. Then she and Mrs Ross settled to an unusual gossip about the accident his father had suffered, and which Donald knew so little about. He listened now, but there was still nothing to get hold of: all the real points had been blunted by time, or use, or by some reluctance to name them. He sat and listened until he almost dropped his saucer, and knew he had nearly fallen asleep. He put the cup and saucer on the table and went on listening to what Mrs Ross had said to herself when the news first came. Donald sensed there was something she was not saying, though he knew he was involved in the matter somehow. Mrs Ross and Mrs Jackson grew smaller and smaller, were a glimmer in the eye, and were no longer there, and in that other place, a cold stable, were forgotten.

"If you have no horses how do you fetch and carry?" old Tarmer was saying.

"We fetch and carry for ourselves," said Jackson, remembering the narrow trails and steep hills, the hidden meadows and high fields of his own country further north. "There's nothing for the horses to eat. We live only in the hills, and there are no valleys like this."

"There's no valley like this," said Tarmer. "Neither as it

58

was before, in the old lord's time, or since this thing came on us."

"The worm?" said Jackson.

"It can hear," said Tarmer. "Say it in other ways, or it will come for you. Four it got in the night, or you wouldn't be here."

"I know," said Jackson. "What else do I have to do?"

"Go on cleaning this harness," said Tarmer. "And anything else he tells you to do, or I tell you to do, or anyone else does. We haven't lost much time. That last lad wasn't here above a week before he had that nightmare."

"Nightmare?" said Jackson. "It had him, you mean."

The old man was rocking to and fro at the jest, pleased at the way Jackson had taken it up, but Jackson felt a little stupid about the way he had done it, by accident. He felt a struggle of shame come over him, and with the struggle there came a glimpse of another place, and for a moment he was Donald and Jackson, something different from Donald Jackson as one person, and he was seeing both places, and could again choose which to take. He chose the one with less shame and guilt to it, and found himself again cleaning harness in a stable.

A bell sounded in the yard outside. Tarmer laid aside the leather he was working on. "You'd better go into the hall now," he said. "They'll be wanting you to serve on or something. After that bell you go in the house for a bit and you come out when dinner's over."

"Good," said Jackson. "I'm a bit hungry."

"Plenty of practice at that," said Tarmer. "You'll not get to eat during daylight, so don't think it. We common people don't, unless you're like me and lay something by." He got up

59

and hobbled into another section of the building, and came back with a bag. From it he brought a flake of bread and broke it in two. "There's no spare today," he said. "But tomorrow and other days don't take and eat all you get when you wake. Lay some by, like us all, for a bait at noon."

"I never had anything this morning I could take away," said Jackson. "It was just a drink."

"Aye, you weren't brought up till late on," said Tarmer. "Get that swallowed and be off in the house, or they'll lay something by for you that's not your breakfast: more your breakback."

"Breakback," said Jackson, with his mouth full of the thirsty bread.

"That's his fancy name," said Tarmer. "They always put on a fancy name, but it does them no good. Breakbone, did you hear the like of it? Snapfinger, that's more like it, with that one. Snapfinger."

While Jackson finished putting the last of the bread in his mouth, and still chewed it, Tarmer set him towards the door he was to use to go into the house. "Straight on," he said, "you'll come to it. They'll tell you what they want. It's too many years since I was at it that I couldn't tell you right for these days if I knew, with all their fancy court manners. It was different before It came."

Jackson walked to the door across the yard and went in. There was a high passage inside with openings to the right and left. He stood and waited, to see what he had to do, when he was told to do it. At first nothing happened, and then there was quite a lot of movement, of men going back and forth across the passage, some walking in a leisurely way,

some hurrying and carrying dishes. The crossing and recross-
ing went on, then stopped, and there was quiet again. Then
a boy came out and looked at him, stepped up to him, then
behind him, and took his arm and bent it behind and made
him walk forwards and through one of the openings in the
passage.

They came into a big kitchen, where there was a fire burning and the smell of food. The kitchen people were eating
round the fire. Jackson was urged to stand beside them, and
they looked at him and went on eating.

"He stinks," said one. "Worm's dung," he added, with a
mouth full of meat. "We can't send him in like that. Get him
out and washed. You see to it, Miral."

Miral was the boy who had hold of him. Jackson waited
until the grip weakened or was less ready and pulled himself
away, but the cook hit him on the knee with a ladle so that he
had to stand on one leg and was caught again. "Get him out,"
said the cook.

"This way," said Miral, and pushed him out through the far
door. This was the biggest building Jackson had ever been in,
and the one with the most rooms. They went along passages and
across internal courtyards, along a battlemented wall top, until
they came to a muddy yard with a well in it. Miral released him
and told him to draw up water with the windlass and fill a
trough. Jackson could see what was to happen and thought
there was no point in fighting against it for the sake of pride.
He filled the trough, and was told to get into it and get some
of the stink off himself.

The air was cold. The water was cold. Jackson shuddered
in both for a time, and then became used to them. Then Miral,

who had been waiting, told him to get out and draw more water, and that bucketful Miral poured over his head.

"What now?" said Jackson.

"I got you out and washed," said Miral. "That's all I had to do."

"What do I do?" said Jackson. Miral was not going to tell him, he found out. He put his clothes back on, and tried to find his way back to a part of the building he knew. Miral watched him from corners, sometimes going round another way and arriving ahead of him.

The bell rang again. Miral went away. Jackson followed a smell of cooking and found himself back at the kitchen again. Now it was empty and the fire had been raked apart and was not burning any more, but the stone of the hearth sent out a big steady heat.

Two old women came gossiping in cracked voices into the kitchen and to the stone bench under the high window. They carried baskets with cloth in and they were obviously sewing women. They took no notice of Jackson, from what he could understand by their speech, but in a little while they had between them found in their baskets red clothes for him. Then they called to him and he went to them, because everybody here seemed to be in charge of him in one way or another.

The clothes were fitted to him, at first pinned round him with black thorns, and then sewn. Then, when the clothes were ready for wearing they were handed to him and the old women went out of the kitchen. Jackson stood by the fire again and put them on.

The lord came in. "Are you ready?" he said.

"Yes," said Jackson. "Where shall I put my old clothes?"

The lord did not seem to hear him, and Jackson repeated his question.

"If you speak like that again it will be the last thing you say," said the lord. "You do not speak to me unless I have spoken to you. You do not ask me questions. I am not your equal. I am your lord. When you are allowed to speak to me you say 'My lord' every time you open your mouth. This may be one of the rottenest posts in the country, but I'm going to administer it properly. You are the first thing that is going to be administered. Throw your old clothes in the back of that fire. Then come with me."

"Right," said Jackson, throwing the clothes on to the embers and getting a mouthful of smoke. "My lord," he added, when he was looked at.

That night he slept in the outer room of the lord's chamber. He woke twice, once when the lord shouted for water, and once when the worm in the hills hooted and vibrated. After each waking he was a long time wakeful before sleeping, because he was cold in the new clothes. The lord, he found, slept in a thin gown with only a sheet to cover him, less than Jackson himself had, with a blanket and a piece of animal pelt about the size of a cat.

"You'll be used to sleeping in a huddle down in the huts," said the lord. "That won't do, Jackson. Out in the field of duty you may have to lie on the ground in the rain, so get used to hard-lying, leave pillows and quilts for the old lords."

"Yes, my lord," said Jackson.

In the morning the lord went down into the town, with Jackson running beside him. The worm had been down again and knocked a hut to pieces. The man and woman in it had run from the creature, but it had touched them and they were expected to die. The worm had eaten two goats instead.

When the lord had inspected the scene he rode round the edges of the town, and then back up the hill to the castle. This time Jackson was ready to take the horse, and knew something about the care of its harness and where to hang each thing. When the bell rang he went in and waited at the table for the lord, and handed dishes.

"There should be a steward to tell you what to do," said the lord. "But things are in such a bad state here that there is nothing there should be. This is a very distant corner of the kingdom, Jackson, and in a very bad state. The people here think the worm is the worst thing, but I think the administration's rotten, there's no staff, there's no one who can read and write in the district, and this has all got to be put right. With a proper administrative set-up the worm would probably leave of its own accord."

Jackson had to fight Miral before the week was out. Miral was jealous of Jackson for having the position of honour, the place that was in some ways the best on the staff. Old Tarmer, cleaning the saddles with Jackson one day, said "I see you won't be doing this for long, boy."

"I shan't mind," said Jackson. "I don't want to be a servant. I wasn't born one, and none of our people serve."

"Not that," said Tarmer. "Servant you are until he sets you free, you can't argue with that. But I hear he fancies you for the service, to come up and be a lord in the end, like him. That's how many of them start, you see, just likely lads. I was one myself, Jackson, but I never came far with it. And Miral's

64

another, but he didn't get fancied either. But the lord seems to take to you, the brisk, bossy devil."

The fight was not fought in the castle but out in the town, on an afternoon when there was nothing to do. It began on the steps of one of the castle postern gates, and went downhill. It began with a battle that seemed to the death, but which never came to death, only to a slow stop, with no winners. Miral was bigger than Jackson, but Jackson had had more exercise recently and could go on hitting hard for slightly longer than Miral. That part of the fight ended in sulky peace and separation. Then it continued later, when Jackson had sat in the road and considered his marks and wounds. It went on until dusk, and both of them ignored the bell that summoned them to return to their tasks.

Miral won in the end, perhaps, knocking Jackson down so that he was unable to find enough resolution to stand up. By this time there were townspeople about and children watching the fight. Miral stood over Jackson, whose head ached and whose limbs would only sprawl when he wanted them to lift him. Miral spat at him and then walked, not very quickly, away through the darkening street towards the castle.

That night Jackson dared not go back to his place. For one thing he had torn his clothes to split shreds down one side of the back. He was afraid of Miral, too, and he was late in any case. Instead of going back he found his way to Carrica's hut. If he had been able to see clearly or walk firmly he would have left the town then, but he was too dizzy.

Carrica said "I have seen you running beside the lord," but she did not know he had been fighting because of the darkness, and they did not talk because of the same darkness, but settled in the hut to silent sleep, and a very uncomfortable night. Bruises grew on him, hard and tender. Scratches and grazes tightened. To be touched woke him, to move himself woke him as well.

It was worse in the morning, because then the deep-bruised muscles spoke up when he walked. But he walked up to the castle, saying to Carrica that he would stay in the lord's service until he had fought Miral and won.

When he came to the castle the lord was on his horse ready to go down into the town on his daily visit. "Come, Jackson," he said, and threw his spear in the usual way. This time Jackson missed it, because he was too stiff to be agile. The lord took no notice of his pains, and set off down the hill at his usual pace, with Jackson jerking beside him, tears of pain coming from his eyes and dissolving what he looked at.

The stars seemed to let more light in than the town days ever afforded. For a moment he was moving in a painful jog and keeping a painful stillness at the same time. Then he was not moving but sitting relaxed and listening to Mrs Jackson and Mrs Ross talking.

"You're nodding, Jackson," said Mrs Jackson. "Donald, I mean. Go to bed."

Donald got up from the chair where something near sleep had come to him, and went to his room. He meant to sit in bed and read the history book, but true sleep came to him and the book slid to the floor.

VI

THE NEXT NIGHT Donald understood that he was to come home and light the fire and find his own tea and then stay in and work until Mrs Jackson came home. "I don't want to have to trail all over the town for you," she said.

"You know where I'd be," said Donald.

"That's another reason," said Mrs Jackson. "You've plenty of opportunity for friends your own age in our own congregation. It's not like it was when we first came here, just half a dozen people in two chapels. It's ten times that number now, and all in one place, more than the church gets. And I'm not saying it to boast, but Daddy and I have had quite a lot to do with the increase in numbers by our work for God. It just seems a little unusual to me that you, of all people, should spend so much time at the vicarage."

"He's not just a friend, he's a way of life," said Donald.

"That's a remark that's very near blasphemy," said Mrs Jackson. "I sometimes wonder whether you ever make any attempt at faith, Donald."

Donald said nothing more. Mrs Jackson put on her coat and they went out of the house together. Now he had come back alone. He took the milk in with him today and closed the door behind him. He had laid the fire before going in the morning and he put a match to it. It was a friend, talking in the grate.

He swept the shiny tiles below the fire and ushered the little heap of dust through a gap at the end of the draught-guard. He dusted his hands, made a face at himself in the mirror on the sideboard, stood on his head in one of the armchairs, and wondered what to do next. The usual thing was homework in his own room. Today he did it on the kitchen table, with the benefit of fire.

Towards tea time he put on the kettle and made tea, eating bread and jam and a piece of crumbly cake. Then he went on working. The fire grew mature and silent, and the house grew silent with it. The quietness overpowered him in time, and he left his books and the fire and went into the garden, hoping to hear news of humanity from the other side of the hedge.

Mrs Jackson came back at the edge of darkness, somewhat the same time as yesterday. He saw her coming up the glade of the hill, and perched more coal on the fire to make it flame, and switched on the kettle, taking his books through to his own room.

"Oh, you are here," said Mrs Jackson. "Good."

"It's what you said," said Donald, hoping to be praised for obedience. Mrs Jackson was tired, though, and thought he was being insolent, and told him it was time he became wiser and more prepared to walk in the ways set before him. Donald went to his cold room and to his work again. Mrs Jackson had her tea and then started the last of the ironing, since she had no books to correct.

The next day was Saturday. In the morning after breakfast Donald finished his week-end homework. Then he was sent to have a bath, but not be long. After that he and Mrs Jackson left together for the bus station, to visit the hospital.

The hospital was a comfortless place, not just because it was unhomely, but because it made Donald uncomfortable. He knew about nurses, as a species of person, but he was not quite prepared for them as real persons present with him, and he did not like the way some of the older ones were having covert conversations with other visitors, and he did not like the visiting feeling of the other people there, in their hats and coats and their own discomfort.

Mrs Jackson was in a bed halfway down the ward, under a window. The air in the room was mixed hot and cold. The hot air brought out the smell of paint, and the cold air made distinct the chemical smells of the ward. From the swing doors at the end came a faded smell of food.

Donald and Mrs Jackson walked down the centre of the ward. Mrs Jackson was used to it. Donald felt that he was in bedroom after bedroom that he had no right to be in, as he passed each bed. Mr Jackson was sitting half up, resting on pillows. His face was fevered and there was sweat on his brow, his hair dampened with it.

He looked at them and said without greeting them, "You've been a long time."

"I'm sorry dear," said Mrs Jackson. "We should have come on the first bus, but Donald had to have a bath."

"Donald," said Mr Jackson, as if Donald were some stroke of fate that had delayed the journey. He did not look at either of them now.

Donald stood at the foot of the bed, feeling the cold metal of the rail with the insides of his fingers and the warm of the blanket with the backs.

"Don't shake the bed so," said Mr Jackson. Donald stepped

away, but in doing so he kicked the leg of the bed. Mr and Mrs Jackson looked at him, and he went into the middle of the ward and got in the way of a nurse with a trolley, who asked him to stay by the patient he was visiting, please. He went back and stood near Mrs Jackson. She was sitting on a chair, holding Mr Jackson's hand, and he was looking at the roof of the ward. They were not talking.

After a time one of the more senior nurses came to Mrs Jackson and asked if she would come and talk to the ward sister. Mrs Jackson got up, and Donald sat in the chair. The nurse smiled at him and said "Is it your grandpa?" and went away.

Donald looked at the man on the bed, who turned his head and looked back at him for a moment, and then turned wearily away. It was a stranger, Donald thought, some one who did not belong to him at all, someone unknown and recently appeared, with whom he had no part. But still, in the run of time, this was the man who had raced about in a wheel chair and made racing car noises to amuse a small boy. Perhaps the small boy was no longer there either, and there were two unacquainted people in this communal bedroom with its separate territories and divisions horizontally into the space under the high beds and the space above, and all the people shared the narrow layer between bed height and a man's standing height.

But this was the racing car man, and this was the small boy, and they did belong to each other, though not across the present, only through each others' past.

Mrs Jackson came back and told Donald to say goodbye for now and wait in the entrance hall of that wing of the hospital. Then she sat down again. The words of goodbye came out of Donald's mouth and were lost in the ward, and not noticed.

He went out of the room, down the stairs, and waited in a lower hall.

In half an hour Mrs Jackson came out again. "He refused his injection," she said. "But he took it in the end, and he was much better for it. He has a great deal of pain. He said he was sorry for not saying much to you, and now he's asleep."

Donald said nothing. A flutter of guilt and gladness and association moved in his throat and squeezed behind his eyes so that they moistened. He swallowed a spasm of muscle that might have been a sob, and walked mistily out of the building beside Mrs Jackson.

They were in the city again, beyond the black stone of the hospital. They went down to the bus station and had lunch there, and then came home in the bus. Mrs Jackson said there was no point in staying because Mr Jackson would be asleep.

"He was worse today," she said. "More pain and more fever."

They got off the bus two villages short of the town and walked three miles back along the lanes, getting to the bungalow without going among the houses. But they had to go on into the town to get some shopping done, so they lit the fire as they went past and came back forty minutes later to find the room warm and that they were already hungry for tea.

"What are you going to do?" said Mrs Jackson.

"I can't go to Berry's because it's Saturday and he does his sermon," said Donald. "I could go and watch Nessing's telly, or he might be going to the pictures." Going to see a film was one of the things that Mr and Mrs Jackson were divided about. Mr Jackson was against them, Mrs Jackson did not mind. So Donald had to arrange matters carefully.

"The other kids have been," said Donald. "A lot have."

"I don't know," said Mrs Jackson. "If Daddy were here I wouldn't mind, probably, would I? And I would arrange it so it would be all right. So I suppose you can go if Nessing is going. I hope I'm thinking right."

"It's what you would say," said Donald.

"Don't credit me with actions that might not be mine," said Mrs Jackson. "It's not a question of right or wrong but the application of principles. I wish I could rely on you more to make the right decisions for yourself, but you don't seem to be able to think things out except with reference to what you want for yourself. You have a heavenly master to make your account to in the end; it's not a question of what I think about things: it's your conscience and your soul."

Donald took his money and went. He did not think that what Mrs Jackson said was true. It was just that so many things had no points of principle attached to them, and there was no way of knowing how they lay morally.

Nessing was sticking pins in his sister, and she was trying to glue the cat to the floor. They both gave up when Donald came, and the cat went to sniff the pins, and, Nessing-like, knocked them all to the floor.

"We're going to stop out most of the night," said Nessing. "My dad's out warming up, you know how he is. But Mum took most of his money round to Berry yesterday, and our dad won't get it from him. Berry's stronger, you know."

"He just naturally is," said Donald.

The went to the cinema. The little sister sat between them, and the Wilbert girls were in front, handing toffees back in all the exciting parts of the film. Girl-like, they were only interested in the romantic parts. Donald decided that Jacqueline Wilbert smelt of snails, but her toffees were normal.

After the film Nessing took his sister off to look for his dad in the pubs. The sister had managed to steal three ashtrays from the cinema. She put them down one by one in the passage on the way out, for people to trip over. At home Mrs Jackson was sleepy beside the fire. She had prepared herself a teaching schedule for the coming week, and another schedule of work that could be done if she still had to be away. They were ready for Donald to take on Monday.

The next day the first bus to the city was not until half past ten. Mrs Jackson went to catch it, but Donald stayed at home, and was told what his lunch was, and his tea. He knew he had next to go to chapel, at eleven. He watched the bus go out, and then began to walk slowly down the road past the church towards the chapel.

He had to pass the vicarage first. Berry was just coming out of the gate, and waited for him.

"Alone again?" he said. "Have you been to see him?"

"Yesterday," said Donald. "It wasn't very nice, you know, Berry. He didn't seem to be glad."

"Poor old son," said Berry. "But if he's ill, and I know he is because I've telephoned the hospital each day, then he might not be up to much conversation. What are you doing now?"

"Going to chapel," said Donald.

"Come to church instead," said Berry, "just for a change. I don't offer you the hospitality of my house without offering you the hospitality of my church as well. But I sometimes ask people to come to church without inviting them home. It depends on the people and what I think of them. Spiritually you're all sinners, but personally some are friends."

"I mightn't do the right things," said Donald. "Kneeling and things."

"It's all in the book," said Berry. "Can't go wrong."

"Can I make up my own prayers?" said Donald.

"Any prayer you don't like the look of as it stands you can alter to suit yourself," said Berry. "No extra charge."

Donald went to neither church nor chapel. He was shy of one because of its strangeness, and shy of the other because he realized there would be questions to answer about Mr Jackson, not just once, but many times. He walked on the empty beach instead, until the church sounded twelve o'clock, when he climbed the promenade wall and up Hales Hill to the house. He looked out from a window there and saw his own trail on the flat sands, where he had dragged his feet and made a huge decorative cross. Freehand, he thought, or free-foot, and not very exact in its limbs. He wondered what burial it might be the sign of. Then he got out the sliced ham and tomato and the potato salad and had his lunch.

He wondered how much alone he was. He was tied to everything that had gone before. Today was one lonely day out of many filled ones. Tomorrow was a school day, with people and noise. Today was a bubble in the solidity of existence. To be truly alone, he thought, you would have to be born an orphan. Then the idea came to him that explained many things. Perhaps he was not the child of the two that lived here. If he had been taken in by them, adopted from some unknown source, that might account for the way he turned out not to please them, and give a reason for the disappointment he often seemed

74

to be for them. Perhaps some simple explanation of that sort covered it all, and as well as explaining the facts of unlikeness made him feel less guilty for not being what they intended him to be. If the man called Daddy was not his father, and the woman called Mum not his mother, then he had no need to feel guilty for no longer loving them as parents.

He was about to consider the matter settled and dissolve himself from obligation to them when there was a tapping on the door.

It was Mrs Ross. "I just popped across," she said, "thinking you might be all alone and that's not nice."

"It depends who you are," said Donald.

"In a very close family like yours," said Mrs Ross, coming in and sitting down, "you're bound to feel alone without the others. How is your father today? Have you heard?"

"I think Mr Braxham said he was still ill," said Donald. "But I don't know whether he rang up today or not. He might do it later, or he might have done it already."

"Well," said Mrs Ross, "I must say your father's a generous man, and lives up to his beliefs, and he's had great trials in the past and more just at present, but I can't say I've ever got on with him really, as a person. I admired him for his daughter's sake. . . . No, I don't mean that. I didn't agree with what he did then, and I wouldn't have done it myself, but I admire his strength in doing it."

"My sister?" said Donald. Mrs Ross thought for part of a second and said, "Yes, though I never think of her as your sister."

"I don't know anything about her," said Donald. "I don't even know what she looked like."

75

"Like you," said Mrs Ross. "She was just about your age."

"I've got a picture that might be her," said Donald. "I'll get it, but don't tell Mum I showed it to you because she doesn't know I've got it."

When he brought the photograph from his room Mrs Ross took it and looked at it, tipping it against the light.

"I don't know," she said, "whether it's your sister or your mother." Donald took it back and put it in his pocket. "They're much the same," said Mrs Ross. "Do you want to come across to our house for tea?"

"I think Mum expects to find me here," said Donald. "Thank you all the same. So I'd better wait."

"Slip across if you feel lonely," said Mrs Ross. "And tidy up your dinner things before she comes in."

When she had gone Donald cleared the table and washed the dishes. Then, for something to do, he went outside and swept the leaves from the drive and from all the pavement outside the house, and gathered them up into a heap in the back garden. As he worked, alone and undisturbed, he thought more of the theory of adoption and where he would have been adopted from, and why hadn't he been told. Mrs Ross's woolly remarks came to mind, how his sister and his mother were much the same thing; and the nurse who had asked if it was grandfather. It was possible, he thought, that Cecily had not been his sister at all, but his mother. Who then could be his father?

Then he was on horseback riding across open land, and beside him rode the lord, Breakbone. The town was two or three miles behind them, and they were following the faded track that led southwards. They had crossed the place where the worm roved,

76

and passed through the lord's fields, where the labourers had saluted them as they passed.

"This was a kept road when I came three years ago," said the lord.

"Yes, lord," said Jackson. "And when I came at the same time from the north I came down the road." The bright un-usual sunshine seemed to lie eternally across the gentle hills. The lord looked far, and saw nothing that he was looking for.

"We shall have to come again tomorrow if we do not meet him today," he said. "Or we can ride on and sleep hard and meet him further away. But if we do that we shall be three days out of the town, and one of us should be there."

One of us, thought Jackson. And when I began I was a little whipped boy with no idea of obedience or service and no notion that lords have to rule by being there and doings things. And now I am in the next but lowest level of the service, and could one day be a lord in my turn, but most likely not and will have to settle for a knight, like the one we are coming to meet.

The new lord had spent a year and half bringing the adminis-tration of the town back into shape. The old lord had died fighting the worm when it first came. After him had come three fresh young lords, each of whom had been taken by the worm. After the third one, no lord had been appointed for some time and there had been no rule and no justice. The new lord had put that right, and had at the same time sent out for a knight to deal with the worm. Knights were trained to fight, he said, and lords were trained to other things as well, and could read and write. Knights were well known to be illiterate. At last a message had come to say that a knight had agreed to tackle the worm, and now they were coming out to meet him.

That day they turned back. The next day, the lord said, Jackson could come out alone, and stay out as long as necessary. "I don't think you'll run away now," said the lord. "Do you remember when I had to lock you up after one of your revolts? You were caught trying to get away through my fields and they tied you up and dragged you back."

"I remember," said Jackson. "I was meant to; but it might be your part to forget it." Then he added "Lord" at the end.

"When you are made knight you may leave off the lord," said his master. "And when we are in the fields or out alone. You know you have my special favour and are my friend, but I cannot allow myself to show it in the town, other than promoting you from boy to squire, and I have done that."

"Yes, you have," said Jackson. "And you have taught me to read and write, so that I can be more than a knight if I go through all the degrees."

"That is a thing for a council to decide," said the lord. Then they were at the town gate and it was opening for them.

The town was walled now, and no dwellings were allowed outside it. There was a gate across the river so that the worm could not venture along its bed. When the wall was first made the lord had tried starving the worm by making sure that nothing living was left outside the walls. But the creature had broken the wall down in a place and entered the town, taking men and eating them, and then, losing its own track, it had knocked down houses and killed more as it struggled a whole night to escape. It had forced its way out at last. Since then food had been left for it each night in a flat field. That was the proper thing to do, the lord said, and trained the worm to come at a given time, and made a battleground ready for any knight who

78

took the job on. "These ways are well-tried and tested," said the lord. "They may seem slow, but there is nothing else to do."

Jackson spotted the knight the next day. He was riding along slowly and keeping watch. His three hounds were at his heels, and they were watching too. A knight in unknown country, with a worm known to be in residence, was prepared all the time.

He was horrified to be met by Jackson in a tunic with no armour of any kind and no dogs to keep watch, and only a light spear and a dagger. He was a little put out to find himself met by a mere squire, as well, but he supposed, he said, that it was better than nothing. Then, as he raised the front of his helmet so that he could hear and speak better, the sunlight spun in front of Jackson's eyes, and he was on the grass at the back of the house, raking leaves. Mrs Jackson was coming in at the drive, and looking pleased to see the tidiness.

VII

"HE DOESN'T KNOW how ill he's been," said Mrs Jackson. "But there was some improvement today."

"How ill was he yesterday?" said Donald. He was washing his hands after moving the leaves. Mrs Jackson was setting the table for tea.

"Quite poorly," said Mrs Jackson. "He was a lot better after the injection, sister said, and he had a better night. I think he doesn't like being in the ward, but he won't say. He finds it hard to love his neighbour when he's in pain."

He, him, thought Donald, letting the towel drink cold water from his hands and turn grey. Who is he? What did Berry mean when he called Nessing a bastard? Did he really mean me, and how would he know if he wasn't my father? Nessing isn't a bastard, he's just one of his family. But whose family am I one of? Is that why Berry is so kind to me and why I wish he could say he was my father, and be my father?

There was no answer in the towel, and none in the tea, and no response from the evening sky.

The next day Mrs Jackson visited the hospital only in the afternoon, during the regular week-day visiting hours. Mr Jackson was no longer on the special visiting list. She came to school for most of the morning, and before dinner went home.

When Donald got in at night he found his tea ready laid for him and a note asking him to light the fire and bank it up if he went to the Youth Guild meeting before Mrs Jackson returned. He was out of the house in a sharp cold rain before she came back, and did not meet her on the way to the Guild. This week it was his own minister, Mr French, who was talking. Towards the end of the meeting Berry came in and said a few words, saying that this was his last visit to the Guild, that he would miss it very much and not be happy to lose his friends, but would he hoped be finding new ones in the next place he went to, without wanting to forget any he already had. Then Jacqueline Wilbert sensing the element of human drama in what he had said, offered him a toffee and they played table tennis again. Donald ignored Jacqueline Wilbert and took the nearest place to Berry.

"When are you going?" he asked, in a pause when someone had lost the ball in the kitchen and was making a great fuss crawling about under the legs of the girls who were making coffee.

"A fortnight yesterday," said Berry. "A week next Monday. I'll miss you particularly, Donald. I'll just write my new address on a piece of paper. It's a pity it's term time, because I'm going there on Thursday to look at the place and you could have come with us and helped with the Tobies."

"I'd have liked that," said Donald. "Why couldn't you have gone during the holidays?"

"By the holidays we shall have settled in," said Berry. "You must come then and stay. Are you coming round to the house now?"

"I'd better go home," said Donald. "Mum hadn't come back

when I left and I have to see to the fire. Really I think I ought to go now."

"On my last day, too," said Berry. "But I'm sure you're right. Drop by and tell me how he is when you get time."

"I'll find some," said Donald. "I can, for you."

Berry took Donald's hand and put something in it, then closed the hand over the thing and squeezed it. It was the warm Wilbert toffee Jacqueline had given him.

When he got home the house was still empty. He made the fire blaze harder and sat beside it. The toffee was still in his hand. It smelt of snails from being Jacqueline Wilbert's, he thought, but Berry had touched it. He unwrapped it sticky from its paper, ate it, and folded the paper up to keep it, putting it with the note in Berry's writing about his address. These were the only things that Berry had ever given him. But perhaps he will write, he thought.

The fire danced away into infinity. The knight was raising his visor clumsily with both hands. His horse's head went down and plucked at the grass growing in the road. The visor came up and the knight rubbed his nose. His face was like a nest of new-born rabbits in a bowl, pink and mobile, fringed in white hair that makes the nest. He looked from side to side over the country.

"I hope you know the habits of your worm," he said. "But I wouldn't go about dressed like that. What sort of worm is it?"

"We sent you a description," said Jackson. He had written it himself, after the lord had decided that the worm did not fit into the ordinary categories and would have to be described in words that fitted only it.

"Yes, of course," said the knight. "I have it with me. We'll

82

go over it, your lord and I, when we get to the castle. How far is it?"

"About three miles," said Jackson. "We'll be quite safe if we're careful. It doesn't come out without making a lot of noise, and we shall hear it, and then it doesn't leave its track."

"Hmn," said the knight. "What rank are you?"

"Squire," said Jackson. "But I expect I'll go on to be a knight."

"It's a way of living," said the knight. "Another year or two and I'll be retiring to a farm, if some worm doesn't get me before that. What establishment has your lord got?"

"Himself and me," said Jackson. "It's a very small place, and we can manage quite well."

"Where did you come from?" said the knight. "Before you came here?"

"I don't know where the lord was," said Jackson. "But I came from the north, and he found me in the town and made me his boy."

"He hasn't any knights of his own, I suppose," said the knight.

"No," said Jackson. "He heard of you and wrote to you."

"I thought there couldn't be any knights on the staff, or you would know how to speak to them, master squire. You must call me sir when you speak, and my name you know, sir Percecoeur."

"I'm sorry, sir," said Jackson.

"And now stop your chatter," said the knight, sir Percecoeur. "We have to listen for this worm."

They rode on in silence, with the three hounds looping the track on either side. The sun, that had been holding still at noon dropped a little way. The knight rode on with his head nodding, held up by the metal of the helmet. Once or twice Jackson noted wheezy snores coming from the helmet. The knight was relying on his hounds to warn him of any danger.

It was the yelp of a hound that woke him. His horse spun under him, his hands went to the visor, and all at once he was safe behind it again, and, presumably, awake.

They were in sight of the town now, or in sight of the cold cloud that hung over it at all times, banking in the valley all the year round. The hound had scented the worm, or its traces.

"It's the track of the worm, sir," said Jackson. "It lies across the hill down there."

"Ride forward and tell me what you see," said sir Percecoeur.

"There's no need," said Jackson. "It's just the same as it was this morning. It hasn't been this way today."

"A knight, on approaching the target, adopts a defensive posture and neglects no precautions," said sir Percecoeur. "He assumes full responsibility for the pursuit of the worm, and for the safety of himself and the local population. He is able to call into service any suitable person, who must then obey lawful and reasonable commands. So go forward, squire, and tell me what you see."

Jackson rode forward, and saw what he expected to see: there was the wide torn track of the worm, broken ground and broken trees, and the stale faded smell that had been there this morning, because the worm had not come this way for almost a week. Nothing had changed during the day. He rode back to sir Percecoeur. Sir Percecoeur was assembling a lance with his gauntleted hands. The hound that had scented the track had sat down by the road a hundred yards from the worm trail, and was sniffing distastefully as the smell came drifting by on small air currents.

"There's the worm's trail, sir," said Jackson. "But it hasn't been this way today, and not for about a week."

"We need not disturb the trail," said sir Percecoeur. "Lead me round another way to the town."

Jackson explained that the trail went all round the town, and that the only way in was across it. Sir Percecoeur could not be convinced at first, although it seemed to be a thing simple enough to understand. At last he agreed to cross the trail, saying that it was a most unusual thing to do, to indicate that humans were showing interest in the worm by going near its roads. Jackson said that people crossed the track every day, going out to work in the fields. Sir Percecoeur thought it was all a very untidy way to behave, and if that was the best they could do no wonder they still had trouble with the creature.

They came down to the track. The hounds had run ahead, and stood on the borders of it, smelling the air and whining. The smell, faint though it was after a week, made their eyes run and their jaws moist.

"Where is it?" said sir Percecoeur. "Show me it." He was at that moment looking across the hundred feet of churned ground. Jackson pointed out to him that this was the trail. Sir Percecoeur sneezed inside the helmet, because the irritant fumes had got in. He lifted his visor and looked more clearly. He had been expecting a narrow path, say eight feet wide, he said. This monstrous spoor was more than he had ever seen in his life. And what was this stink?

Jackson said it was old worm stink. He did not notice it

himself any more, and assumed it was there. Fresh worm stench he could be aware of, but this old trail was so usual that it was hardly there.

"Well, forward," said sir Percecoeur. Jackson rode ahead, and waited for the knight. Two of the hounds came forward when the knight told them, but the third would not stir on to it. One of the hounds got to the far side with Jackson, but the second stopped halfway and lay down. Jackson rode out to it, dismounted, and picked it up. It lay across the neck of the horse with bulging eyes and heaving ribs. He put it on the ground beside the one already across, and then rode back to the knight. He had not been able to start across the trail. His horse refused to walk on that ground.

"It's no damn use," said sir Percecoeur after a time. "If it won't it won't. I don't know what hellish monster you have here, squire, but this is the first time my horse has refused like this. We'll have to go round another way."

There was another way, of course. They followed the outside of the trail down towards the sea. The hounds on the far side, both now recovered, went with them thirty yards away, now and then running a little way into the broken ground, but never getting across. The knight grew more and more out of temper. The trail, he said, was the same width all the way along. How wide was this worm? he asked.

"It's only about a third of this width," said Jackson. "It just doesn't walk very tidily, that's all. It doesn't go straight, but in waves, from side to side."

"It's too big," said sir Percecoeur. "I don't like it."

They came to the sea. Here the track crossed the sand, and the tides had washed a clean stretch, so that there was a gap in the circuit at the mouth of the river. To get into the town, whose walls were on the cliff, they had to ride up the river, a very strange procedure, Jackson thought, and to the river gate. There Jackson had to shout until someone heard them and men came to withdraw one of the stakes of the barrier. They rode up the water, all three hounds with them now, and climbed up the bank and were met by people.

Jackson was ashamed of their way of entry. He led the way up the streets to the castle, and into the courtyard.

There was more trouble here. The castle dogs woke up at once and set on the three hounds. The hounds were not fighters, but they could run. Two of them ran out into the town and the third was cornered by two enemies. Men came out to separate them, Miral and the lord himself. The two that had got away were howling in the streets outside.

Sir Percecoeur lifted himself heavily from his horse, put up his visor, and stumped to the gate, where he stood whistling until his own hounds returned. Behind the hounds came townspeople with the castle dogs on thongs. The knight looped his own leashes to his hounds, and came back to the third one, which the lord was leading to him. Sir Percecoeur took the animal without thanks. "Take my horse in," he said to the lord. "And bring my bags to the hall." Jackson ran up and took the horse, but the knight said, "No, not you. You take me to my lodging and get my armour off me."

"Go on, squire," said the lord. "Don't make a fuss."

"No, indeed," said the knight. "Bring my bags to me at once, groom," he said to the lord.

Jackson led him to the room on the gallery at the end of the big hall. It was the best room they had. The knight looked at the fire but did not go near it yet. Hot armour is too hot. Jackson unlaced him, picking at the knotted leather with fingers and teeth until the firm plates slackened and could be removed. The armour was common black, rubbed and rusty but thick. It was the sort that a working knight could look after for himself without much trouble. The lord's armour, down in the hall, was gilded at its edges and certain plates were set with enamel, and the breastplate had a let-in silver design that had to be cleaned often, and the whole suit was polished bright with sand and oil. Some of the company knights, the lord had said, who rode in bands, had very fine armour indeed.

The armour came off sir Percecoeur and lay unevenly deflated on the bed. Jackson set it on the stand piece by piece, and the knight went to the fire. Out of the black suit he was a small, elderly man with a big nose and teeth with ragged edges, which showed that he had been a knight's boy once and had to take armour of his own master.

"Is this all the attention I get?" he said. "I expect more than this, and I usually get it."

"I'll send Miral, sir," said Jackson. "He's meant to look after you, but I think the dogs bit him."

"Your dogs, not my hounds," said the knight. The hounds had come in with them, and were already by the fire, after tangling their leashes up. The knight kicked them aside and sat on a stool, taking up the leashes and easing out the tangles.

Jackson nodded in a half bow, not knowing what was required of a squire to a knight, and went out. Miral was down in the hall, and the sewing women were tearing a piece of cloth to bind up his left arm, where a dog had ripped the skin down. He and Jackson were not friends in any way, but Miral was still employed as a boy about the castle, and Jackson had gone up one degree of rank, so they could not fight and they could not be companions. Miral had attempted once to become a squire by learning the right things, but he had always fallen away from his intention and gone back to being a general help. Jackson could have given him orders if he had needed to, but he knew that would bring trouble in some way.

Miral went up to the knight's room. Jackson went out and washed the day's dust from his hands and face, and walked out across the yard to see that the horses were all right.

Sir Percecoeur came down after a time and went out himself to see that his own horse was well looked after. He came back looking a little startled. When the lord came in he began an apologetic speech about mistaking him for the groom. The lord said that here they had to do everything for themselves, and that at the time he had been groom to a visiting knight who had had a long journey, and what about some ale?

"I suppose there isn't a spot of wine, sir?" said the knight. But there was no spot of wine, because there was no trade in and out of the town.

After supper the lord said that everything was ready for a first view of the worm, if his guest was ready.

"That's the proper procedure," said sir Percecoeur, reluctantly. "Some people wait a day or two."

"Everything's ready," said the lord. "We can't get close enough in broad daylight, but there's a moon tonight and we should be able to see well."

"I'll just have a look at the description you sent me," said the knight. He sent Miral up to his room for the letter the lord had sent him, and looked at it by the candle light. But it was quite clear that he could not read at all, and did not know whether the writing went up and down or across the page. "Yes, yes," he said. "Now about the fee."

"We can show you that too," said the lord. "In gold, as usual."

"I'll just get my things on," said sir Percecoeur. "Come on, boy." He walked up to his room with Miral following. His three hounds followed him up.

"What do you think, Jackson?" said the lord.

"He'll get killed," said Jackson. "I don't really know, but I don't think he wants to fight."

"I don't think he'll get killed," said the lord. "But I bet he wishes he could read. Someone told him the address and the fee, and that's all he knows."

"We told him everything," said Jackson.

"We're all right," said the lord. "He can't complain to the council about anything."

They went out on horseback. The knight borrowed a horse, because his own would never stand the smell of the worm, and they went out of the north gate.

The feeding ground was a little way up the valley. On the side of the hill above it there was a stand of trees too large for the worm to knock down easily. Between the trees the lord had erected palisades to provide extra shelter. From here, if the wind was blowing away from the feeding ground, the lord and Jackson had often watched the worm feeding. Tonight there was a cast cow tethered in the feeding ground, on the clean patch of grass round the stake that the worm did not smear with its slime. The cow stood with its head low, coughing with the stench, which was always fresh in that place.

"Never smelt anything like this, never," said the knight.

"When you're ready we'll call it," said the lord. "It'll come some time during the night in any case, but if we call it it comes sooner."

It was a cold night. Jackson heard the old man's armour rattle against itself (Miral must not have tightened it enough). He drew a breath, raised the trumpet to his mouth, and blew a long croaking blast. The worm did not respond to a pure call, but liked something similar to its own utterance.

A moment later there was a reply, sirening out of the hills.

"Interesting," said sir Percecoeur. Then they settled to wait in silence.

The smell came first. Then, in the dark clearing there was something like a light shadow. There were no distinct edges to moonlight and dark down in this valley. The moon had to shine through the perpetual overcast, touching the earth in a dim radiancy not in beams of light.

The shape in the clearing came larger, and shrank again. The worm moved by contraction, coming in on its own substance, then stretching out its front part, halting that and bringing the rear part up to it. It was so long that there were always three waves of movement along its length. To watch it taking a long walk over the hills was to see it apparently walking through hoops of itself as successive crests rose and sank and stayed still while the substance flowed through.

It came on, screwing its way towards the cow. It was about ninety feet long, of a white colour, limbless, and had two protuberances, one either side, about half way along itself. The head was a searcher on a thick neck. The mouth opened and closed in time to its movements forwards. Its eyes were not plain to see, but it had been proved to possess sight, and a sense of smell and it could hear. More than that, it could sense people who were out of sight, not moving and downwind of it, so that it had an extra sense of detection.

It approached the cow. The cow bellowed and tried to run, but the rope held it. The worm opened a mouth with a ten foot jaw, cast out a clasp of vapour that sparkled in the moonlight, and took the cow in. Then it stood still. The cloud of vapour hung in the air, then fell in a white drift to the ground. The worm lifted its head, made a movement of its neck, and spat something out.

"Skin and horns," said the lord. "Bleached white. You go and look in the morning. Now we'd better wait until we see which way it's going. It comes down to the town and tries to get in, but if it's had food it doesn't bother. When it gets to be too much of a nuisance we have to give it two cows one night, and then it stops bothering us for a bit."

In a while the worm sniffed the air, and took its sacklike way across the river and up the opposite hill. The party of watchers went back the way they had came, and into the castle again.

"I won't take my armour off," said sir Percecoeur. "I'll just get warm, and then I think I'll go out and scout around, you know, now I know a bit about the thing."

"Tomorrow would do," said the lord. "Get more used to its ways."

"Seen enough to have some notion," said the knight. "We'll just have a little drink, what, and see what the night brings, eh?"

In the morning there was no sign of him. He had gone out,

said the gate-keepers, with the lord's horse, and his three hounds on leashes, and had not come back.

Jackson reported this to the lord. "Poor fellow, would you say?" he asked Jackson.

"We'll find his armour somewhere," said Jackson.

"I wonder," said the lord. He and Jackson went out for a look, not up the valley where the worm had roamed that night, but down by the sea. The worm had not been there. But a mile down the strand they found, under the cliffs, the tracks of a horseman and a number of dogs.

"It was too much for him," said the lord. "Do we report him to the council, or do we say that he is unaccounted for after setting bravely out on a mission."

"He's stolen a horse," said Jackson.

"And if he was killed on duty we still pay the fee to his family," said the lord. "I think we'd better say he refused the mission, because I suppose the council will never hear of it. We've lost half a horse, you might say." So they looked at the string of hoofmarks lying under the cliffs, pictured the black-armoured knight hurrying away, and turned towards the town again. The sea spun against Jackson's eyes, turned red, and became the fire in the kitchen. Donald blinked. Outside he heard Mrs Jackson pause at the door and look for her key. He opened the door, and she stepped in.

"I had to stay," she said. "Have you been all right? We'll both have to go in tomorrow, Donald. They think he may not get better."

VIII

IN THE MORNING before breakfast Mrs Jackson went out and telephoned the hospital. Donald watched her walking up the hill again and had tea made when she came in.

"He's much the same," said Mrs Jackson, "but they still want me to go in this morning, even though he hasn't got worse. I think you might as well go to school this morning and come this afternoon on the one o'clock bus. There's not much point in making you hang about all day, and it can't be very interesting for you. I wish you weren't so indifferent these days, Donald."

"The days are just happening," said Donald. "I can't do anything about them."

"Perhaps not," said Mrs Jackson. "We'll tidy up before we go."

Donald took a note to school about the day's plan. He had the headmaster's spoken sympathy, and unspoken sympathy from other members of staff, without wanting either kind. The days were just going on independently, as he had said, and their content seemed hidden by some protective glaze that kept their livingness away from him. He ate his school dinner, then came out of the building alone and through streets that should have shared his liberation from lessons. But the streets were independent too, and he walked alone to the bus, and sat alone in it until he got to the city bus station. Mrs Jackson had come down to meet him, in the space between visiting hours. They walked to the black building and went in.

Mr Jackson was lying down this time, and the pillows had been taken away. He moved his head a little when Donald and Mrs Jackson came to his bedside, even lifting it an inch or two up to see them better. It was not so weary a movement as he had made the last time Donald was here.

"Hello, boy," said Mr Jackson, in a slow drawling tone. "Where's Cecily?"

"She's all right," said Mrs Jackson. "She couldn't come today."

"Is she in another ward?" said Mr Jackson. "She couldn't be in here."

"She couldn't come in today," said Mrs Jackson, calmly.

"Donald," said Mr Jackson, and then he made some noises that were dreadful to hear and made Donald's skin crawl and Mrs Jackson startled. But Mr Jackson was smiling, and he had made the noises on purpose. Mrs Jackson realized what he was doing.

"Oh," she said, in a tolerant, motherly way, "you two are playing racing cars again."

"Brrrrm brrrm," said Donald, making racing car noises quietly, so that other patients would not hear. Mr Jackson replied with his noises, and then stopped.

"Is it a boy or a girl?" he said.

"It's a boy," said Mrs Jackson.

"It's a girl called Cecily," said Mr Jackson, and he laughed. Then he asked again whether it was a boy or girl, and Mrs Jackson said it was a girl.

"Call it Cecily," said Mr Jackson. Then he put up a thin white hand and pushed his hair back, closed his eyes, and went to sleep.

Donald drew away from the bedside. For him the day had begun to be real in a hateful way; the nonsense that was being talked was unbearable nonsense.

Then he was sitting on the floor of the great hall, and the ward of the hospital, much the same size, altered its dimensions a little and turned to sandy stone. He was thinking of his first view of the knight in black armour, and how his face had emerged like the small kernel of a nut from the shell of the helmet.

"We'd better go out and see what it's doing," said the lord. "It's probably the knight's trail we saw on the beach, but we could be mistaken. There might be a bundle of armour and teeth lying out on the hill somewhere. I'll have to write down what happened in the record book, though I don't think any-one will look at it for a dozen years. We'd better be certain."

Jackson yawned, and would have preferred to sit by the fire for longer. But they had to go by daylight, so he said "Yes, lord," and stood up.

They followed the fresh trail of the worm, from where it had left the feeding place, up on to the opposite hill, then down towards the town wall, which it had battered a little before going away into the hills again.

"Better see to that tomorrow, squire," said the lord, looking at the shifted stonework at the foot of the wall and the moved timber above.

"It'll be needing two cows soon," said Jackson, "do you think, lord?"

They both looked at the amount of damage the creature had done, and thought that the worm would need a double meal in about three night's time, going by their experience of its habits.

"We shall have to write off again for a knight," said the lord, when they turned away from the wall. They rode up the hillside, through the people returning from the fields. They followed the worm trail to the hill top, without finding any trace of sir Percecoeur, and then went along towards the creatures lair.

"The wind's our way," said Jackson. "And the ground's warm, so it won't know we are here."

"We'd better have a look at it," said the lord, "and make sure."

The worm lay like a gigantic maggot in the icy bed it had made for itself over the years. The wind blew cold from the place, and the smell crept against eye and mouth and skin. The worm was asleep, with its head laid out on a snow-covered slope. The snow was the condensation of its own breath. During its time here the grain of all that breathed frost had mounted into a hill of solid grey ice, and the worm had worn a single passage down the hillside through it. It lay in a great smoothed cup of the same ice, partly domed in the same substance.

"It didn't have him here," said the lord. "There's no sign."

To make sure finally they rode back to the feeding ground and examined the rejected bundles that lay there. The bundles would decay quickly, becoming a little mound in a week. Last night's bundle was still where it had been cast. Jackson cut it with his sword, to be sure, and noted the whitened horn and hair and hide of its contents, and the white fibre that was the hay the cow had eaten, rejected too by the worm.

"We can be sure now," said the lord. They rode back to the town, partly in the river to clear the worm taint from the legs of the horses. They went in at the north gate. When they were inside Jackson turned to the right to see about one of his daily duties, the warning of the ward elders whose turn it was to provide the worm's meal that night. The town was divided into five wards, each of which provided the meal for one night each week. The lord provided it for the remaining nights. The south river ward was liable for duty tonight, and Jackson found the elder and told him, in case he had forgotten. Then he rode up to the castle, with nothing more left to do but see that the cow, or whatever it was, had been taken down in the twilight before it was quite dark. Sometimes he went, sometimes the lord, and occasionally Miral had been given the duty when it was the lord's turn.

When he got back to the castle the lord was recording in the book the experience with sir Percecoeur. Jackson helped with that, and countersigned the record. The lights were brought, and the day was over. Jackson forgot the matter of the south river ward's duty, and since no one came to the castle to tell him the men were ready to leave, and since he had already in his mind a memory of going to the feeding ground, the matter stayed forgotten.

During the night the worm breached the wall where it had weakened it the night before, got into the town, took its fill of people, touched others with its frozen sides, and went out again.

Jackson was woken by the bell, and went down at once by the light of smoky flares to the crushed houses and shouting people and the gap in the wall. But there was nothing to be done. Beyond the mist of the town there were clouds covering the moon, and there was no light in the land outside. A mile away the worm screamed, and down the river floated the mortal bundles that had once been men and women and children.

Jackson looked at the scene, bitter at himself. He waited until the elder of the south river ward came near, and asked what had happened. It seemed that the ward had been unable to provide what was wanted that night, and the elder had waited until Jackson came down from the castle ready to lead them to the feeding ground. Jackson had not come by nightfall, and then it had been too late to do anything.

"Fool," said Jackson, though he knew he should not speak so to an elder, slightly higher in rank than a squire; and he was as much a fool himself. "If you had come to the castle we could have commuted your payment and provided the beast."

"But you did not come, squire," said the elder. "And you always have before."

"You had better come up to the castle," said Jackson. "If you tell this story to your people (because the worm had come into the south river ward) they may kill you. I should have come, no doubt, but equally you should have sent for me."

The man walked up the dark streets beside Jackson, and they came to the castle.

"We were three days out," said the lord. "It was hungrier than we thought. But always before we have been able to tell. Perhaps it is about to lay an egg."

"It was not fed, lord," said Jackson. "This elder and I are both to blame."

"I see," said the lord. "Accidents will happen, and I will blame no one, because you know your own guilt, and no one is without guilt. The elder had better stay in the castle, and in

99

the morning I shall see what I can do to have the blame forgotten. Squire, stay here with me. We have things to think of now."

The elder went, and Jackson stood by the fire.

"There is nothing to be done tonight," said the lord. "Tomorrow may be different."

"I was at fault, lord," said Jackson.

"The old lord, who had been here for so many years," said the lord, "had this castle and the town and the country round about by inheritance of office, and his family had ruled it for years. He was not a great lord, and not skilled at ruling, and if he had had to work his way up from boy to squire to knight to being a lord he would still be a boy, like Miral, who is one of his natural children. The people knew him, and that made him a good enough lord. I began as the son of a knight, I was a boy in another household, and because I showed promise I was a squire at the court and served several members of the council. I was a knight for two years and then became a lord and was given lands to rule. However, I made a mistake, far worse than yours, a mistake about obeying the ordinary rules of government, and I lost the town to an enemy. I was defeated in the field of battle when there was no need. Lords are not brought to any trial, but I found I was not appointed to a new lordship, I had nothing to live on, and I had to earn a disgraced sort of living as a knight, until this small town was offered to me by kind friends. It's the only place you know, Jackson, but it is far from being the only place in the world. I may never be offered any other place better than this; I may end my days here, a very long way from the noble friends of my youth. But when I was young and a squire I think life was too easy for me, the responsibilities at court are not real, and were not taken seriously. Mistakes were of no importance. If mistakes had been important then, and I had made a few, I might not have made a big mistake later, when it was truly important. So I do not think badly of your mistake, though it is nevertheless a real one, and a failure of duty. It will not stand in your way, and will not hinder your rise to knighthood at the proper time, whenever that is."

Jackson was silent, then turned away and went to his bed, blamed, forgiven; chided, spared. The lord kicked the fire and the sparks chattered up the chimney.

In the morning there was a crowd outside the castle gate, shouting and throwing stones. The stones, however, bounced off the wood and into the crowd again.

"Another rising against us," said the lord, when Jackson brought him water and towels. There had been risings before, at the time when the town wall was to be built and ground was taken from its owners and given to the people who had lived outside before. There had been a big riot when the town was divided into its five wards, and several days' trouble when the arrangement for feeding the worm was told to the people. On that occasion the lord had had to go out in armour and use his sword on the mob. Three bodies were thrown to the worm that night.

"It's still a good sign," said the lord. "When I came here they couldn't have got together to do anything. I expect they will go away before long."

The crowd did not go away. They stayed all day. For a time they tried to batter down the gate, but the matter was too difficult for them to organize and they battered each other instead and two bruised men were sent to the infirmary and the nurses were called. Inside the castle the lord had the windows blocked and the doors barred, brought the horses in under the tower, and watched the town from there. Outside, the townspeople gathered up wood, taking it even from the town wall, and built a scaffolding up the castle wall, until they could look over the top.

"Jackson, go down, and let in a leader," said the lord. "It is time to talk."

Jackson had done this before. It meant standing with his sword bared by a narrow postern in the gate itself, and having stones thrown at him until the people realized that he had come to parley. Then a long time would go by while the crowd calmed itself and began to elect itself a leader, and the children would come and dare each other to touch the sword.

This time it was different. The leaders were already there, and stepped through the gates at once, four of them, two elders and two big fellows.

The lord spoke with them in the middle of the yard. Outside the crowd pounded the gate. "Tell them I cannot hear until there is quiet," said the lord. "And there will be a levy on the town to repair the gate."

One of the elders, escorted by Jackson, spoke to the people outside, and there was no more battering or shouting. The parley in the yard continued.

The complaint was about the worm's attack, about the impossibility of feeding it for much longer, about the failure of sir Percecoeur, and about the town wall itself, which was not strong enough. The lord said it would be stronger if pieces had not been taken from it that very day to build a useless scaffolding up the castle wall. As to sir Percecoeur, he had judged the worm was too much for him to handle, and had returned to his own place, unpaid. The deputation insisted that he must have disturbed the worm to make it so savage, and wanted to have him out and hang him. The lord laughed at them then, and said it was impossible to hang a knight or to kill him in any way but fair combat.

"What about hanging a lord?" said one of the four men.

"That could never be hidden," said the lord. "The council and the court would come and there would be punishments too dreadful to be mentioned." Then, when the general anger had worn off the four men they all went into the hall and Jackson brought out the book that listed each family and its property and cattle. The elder from the south river ward was brought to the meeting, and all the afternoon the richness of the town in terms of eatable meat was gone into, family by family, animal by animal.

"It is clear," said the lord, when they had finished, "that there are three choices. We can go on as we are for the winter, and there will be nothing in spring. We can go without meat ourselves, or we can feed the worm on men and women, a thing that is often done."

"There is a fourth thing," said one of the elders.

"There is a fourth thing, indeed," said the lord. "That I shall do that other part of my duty and kill the worm myself. So that I shall do tomorrow. But I will not risk my life for a town that is not peaceful and well-armoured itself, whose walls are not secure and whole, and whose citizens are not well-governed among themselves."

The deputation went out of the gate and it was closed behind them. The lord went up the tower and Jackson went with him. Neither spoke for a long time. Then the lord said, not the grave words that Jackson expected, but, "From here I can hear them talking in five different places round the castle, telling them what I have promised."

He was listening with a purpose, Jackson thought, and he knew the reason was a good one when he heard the people begin to cheer.

"I have done the right thing," said the lord. "Now we shall begin to make ready, squire," and he smiled an ironical smile that made Jackson look out over the town in case his eyes blinked or wept.

The town and the sky went, and instead of the hanging cold of the top of the tower there was the thick ward air round Donald. Mrs Jackson was saying to him, "It is the drugs that make him slow and wandering, Donald, not any illness. They make him drowsy too. He does not want to appear like this, and we shall never tell him how he was. He would rather not have the injections, but it is impossible not to have them."

Mr Jackson dozed a little and woke a little. He talked of catching a train, and he asked after Cecily again, and after Donald, and did not know him. Donald sat by him, and sometimes stood, and was miserable because of the other people in the ward, because of his own inadequate appreciation of what was going on, and because he was frightened of this head on the pillow saying things he had not heard before in a slow unknown voice. They stayed beyond the normal visiting hour, and when they left Mr Jackson told them to go and see Cecily and tell her it was all right about the train and that there was no need to worry.

"Why does he talk about trains?" Donald asked, when they were in the bus on the way home.

"Because the accident was a train accident," said Mrs Jackson. "You know that surely. That's what hurt him. And it was such a slight accident really, and you know what it did."

"No one told me," said Donald.

"Yes, yes, they did," said Mrs Jackson. "You have forgotten, that's all." Then she was silent, and the bus lurched out into the country. Donald sat silent beside her, with his school books on his knee and the smell of the hospital still lurking on the cloth of his raincoat.

IX

IT MIGHT HAVE been easier for Donald if he had refused to go to the hospital at all the next morning. Mrs Jackson had been out and telephoned and heard the amount of news that did not make her any more or less grave, and said they had better both go in, it wasn't as if Donald were a child. Donald thought he was somebody's child, but not, certainly not, the son of him in the hospital. But every time he thought that, the shame of having to think it sickened him, and he turned away, to think about almost anything else.

Berry was on the bus to the city. Donald smelt the clean church smell move past him. Berry sat three seats ahead and did not look round. Donald remembered that today he was going to his new place to look at it. He envied him a fresh start, and wondered where Mrs Braxham and the Tobies were.

Berry was one of the last off the bus, waiting for everyone else. Mrs Jackson and Donald were away before Berry saw them. He did not see them even when he caught up with them and passed them in the street. He halted when Donald called his name, and then walked with them.

"Hello," he said. "You're early about. I was just going in to ask about your husband, Mrs Jackson, and one or two others who are sick."

"He's about as they expect," said Mrs Jackson. "Thank you, Mr Braxham. We're waiting for him to take a decided turn one way or the other, but at present he is just very ill, and there would be no point in visiting him, Mr Braxham."

"But if there is anything, you will let me know," said Berry.

"Yes," said Mrs Jackson. "Good morning, Mr Braxham."

Berry went on ahead. "He's a pleasant, brainless, good man," said Mrs Jackson. "And he infuriates Daddy because of it. And he acted in a most improper way when he first came to the parish. And I don't think he's aware of it, fully. But he's going soon, so I don't have to worry about it with you."

Donald had been listening and not listening. The black building had been growing larger and larger ahead. Donald knew that it contained, in all its bulk, only one living thing, some centre, some patch of life. That patch of life was not even a person at present, not even intelligence, and most of all it had nothing to do with his own existence, he had nothing to do with its; he had no feelings about it except revulsion.

He stopped on the stairs leading to the ward. After the revulsion came guilt and then a wild wordless frustration putting him beyond the power of thought. He was not ready, this morning, to look at the man in the bed, nor was he able to explain. He turned and ran down the stairs, and at the bottom of them stopped, feeling he could do so in safety for long enough to call up to Mrs Jackson, "I'm not going in, I can't."

Mrs Jackson looked down on him, poised as if she would walk down to him, then turned and went up the stairs. Donald did not watch her go, but went out of the building and looked at the scant city grass on the sooted earth.

There was a hand on his shoulder. It was Berry's hand, and

that face looking down at him. "Won't they let you in this morning?" said Berry.

"I couldn't go again," said Donald. "I won't ever go in again, him, and the place, and the illness. I don't want to die in an illness."

"No," said Berry. "Stay here a minute, my dear boy. I just have one more word to say to a rather fierce sister, and then I'll be out here again. I can think of several things to do."

Donald went on looking at the grass, then found he was seeing more, and looking at the rails between the grass and the street, and then at the street and the houses beyond. There seemed now that there was more world available than the bed in the building behind, and more people than lay in the bed.

Berry came back. "We'll move straight off," he said. "Left right, left right, Donald. I've sent a message up to your mother, telling her I've got you for the day, and I've found that your father is ill, but not giving much cause for alarm, and they like your mother to come in because it makes him happy and easier to manage, and the sister says you obviously don't gain much from your visits and might as well be out of the way until he's a little better."

"Sister?" said Donald, puzzled for a moment.

"Big chief nurse," said Berry. "Waving heap big bed-pan and indecent little pee-bottle and sending innocent probationers to jab blunt needles into frail patients' unsuspecting bums at five in the morning."

"He wouldn't have injections," said Donald.

"That was on principle, founded on inspiration," said Berry. "God knows what the inspiration was founded on."

"God was meant to know," said Donald.

"Perhaps he did," said Berry. "But for ordinary people inspiration is not enough, we don't inspire deeply enough, we've got to act in an unmindful way, almost, and carry out our duties, and realize that against the established world we have to put an established church, corporation against corporation, because in the end one or another will take over, and there has to be a structure, a recognized way of doing things."

Then Berry's voice, walking along a city street as flat as milk, became one with the lord's voice, walking with Jackson down the steeper hills of the town. For a time Donald felt the vertiginous pull of both tilts, while retaining his own uprightness. The lord and Berry were talking about the same thing, the need for a structure of government, a law of ruling, an accepted way of doing things, a framework in which to live and achieve the best.

"You will have to rule," said the lord. "You are the only person, dear boy, who knows how to. You are the only person who can read and write well enough. You're the only person with enough wit and will."

"But you aren't dead yet, lord," said Jackson. "And my wit and will and service are yours, not the town's. I'm your squire, and I serve you first. I don't care about the town, but I do care about you."

"That's quite right," said the lord. "And my devotion is to the king and the court first, and the town second. That's a principle of government. But you know all these things, and you know that I could be killed this afternoon, Jackson, and that if I am then someone will have to carry on, and that person is you. And now I'll set about organizing the fight."

They were on the way to see about certain matters now. It was proper for the fight to be witnessed by the elders of the community, and as many more as possible, from a safe place. So the town wall was being strengthened at the point nearest the feeding ground, and people were already squabbling for the best places. Jackson had to be there for a time and settle who went where. The job became easier, because, before he chose one person or another they were all against him, but as soon as he let them through they were on his side. He warned them that a dozen people might be called to assist the lord on the field of battle, by helping him on to his horse if necessary, or bringing him a new horse, or lances and spears as required, and recover his body if the worst happened to him. In spite of the possibility of this grim duty the wall filled up.

The lord and squire went into the castle to prepare themselves.

"At this point, usually," said the lord, "the champion gets drunk enough not to care, but only if he knows it's a hopeless battle is he drunk enough to fall off his horse. If I get drunk enough to fall off the horse you have to strap me on."

But the lord had no intention of drinking anything but water. Instead of worrying about the battle ahead he sent for the books of town and castle, and looked at them as if it were his monthly check, a week early. Then he signed the sheets, and closed the books.

"I'll put them away," said Jackson.

The lord put his hand on the record book. "Wait a minute," he said. "Miral can put them away later."

"Miral's only a boy," said Jackson. "He isn't meant to touch the books."

"We shall have to make him a squire," said the lord. "And since we are rapidly coming to the field of battle, I shall be able to adopt an emergency procedure with you, Jackson, and promote you to field-knight before I go to fight. I can't make you a full knight, but I can make you a half one, now that there is an emergency."

"I'm not ready for that," said Jackson.

"How often do I give you orders?" said the lord.

"Not very often," said Jackson. "Not since I stopped disobeying them. I think your last order was to tell me not to go down and sleep in the huts, when there were huts."

"It made you stink," said the lord. "And divided your loyalty, because there was a girl down there, and I wasn't going to share you with a girl. Squires are not much good once they have their minds on girls."

"Carrica was her name," said Jackson. "She found enough money to commute her field service and work in town, and I got her a place in the infirmary."

"You don't have to tell me," said the lord. "Get Miral."

Jackson got Miral, who came in with a greasy apron, and was made to take it off. "You're appointed to the rank of squire," said the lord. "If I'm killed you'll be squire to the acting lord, who will be Jackson here, appointed field-knight in combat conditions. So go and get clean and be ready to come down to the field."

"Do you know," said Jackson, when Miral had gone, "when you've killed the worm there won't be much to do here. We could leave, and Miral could take over. We've only to get his mother to say who his father was, and he can be lord in his own right."

"We'll have left the books in order," said the lord. "We'll set out, perhaps, who knows?"

But now it was time to go the shorter journey to the place of battle. Armour had to be put on first. Miral was called back to help, but Jackson checked each loop and tie. It was a quiet process, turning the friend and lord into a bulky anonymous figure, at first seeming bigger than the man had been, and then, when Jackson was used to the size of the moving armour, it seemed that the man looking out from it had shrunk.

They took him to his horse and put him on it. Jackson took the trumpet to call the worm with, and they came out of the castle gate.

There were waiters and watchers here, all silent. The whole town had fallen quiet. Miral was last in the procession, leading two spare horses and supporting two lances and a bundle of spears. Jackson was next ahead, with a spare sword. At the front rode the lord, lanced and sworded and gauntleted. They rode down by the stand. Here the lord chose men from the watchers, and they scrambled out across the benches. They were likely to be killed, much more so than the lord was. He had taken that into account, Jackson thought, and chose a quarrelsome elder and two troublemakers among the dozen. Then, with that done he gathered them all round him and told them how to dispose themselves and what their duties were.

Then he dropped his visor and saluted the town. The people, who had been silent, cheered back at his salute and then went on talking. The three horsemen, five horses and twelve men walked towards the feeding ground. The men went into the wood. Miral and the horses went to the edge. The lord rode to the middle of the feeding place and inspected the ground.

He called men forward to clear away some irregularities, mostly bundles of cow skin in various sorts of decay. Then he had them dig earth from a bank and scatter it where the ground was still either slightly frozen or slippery with slime. Then, when he was satisfied with the ground he signalled to Jackson, who rode ahead of him and up the valley for a hundred and fifty yards, and blew the trumpet.

Ninety seconds later there was reply. At this reply Jackson turned. Combat had started, and he came at once to the lord, dismounted, and knelt in the scattered earth. The lord said, lifting out his sword, "In the hour of battle and in expectation of death I give you, Jackson, the rank of field-knight, to acquit you in battle, to honour you in trial and fit you for the king's service where it pleases him to send you. Rise, sir knight."

Jackson stood up, a knight. "Mount quickly," said the lord.

"Yes, sir," said Jackson. He need not call him lord now, since their ranks were not far apart. He mounted, turned back towards the lair of the worm, and rode forward a good way. He and the lord had made the plan this way. He blew the trumpet again, and heard the worm respond, and knew how far away it was.

The horse trembled. It had smelt and heard, and now it saw the worm shifting its bulk along. The worm saw horse and man and altered its line of movement. Jackson watched it approach and hasten, then turned the willing horse and galloped back towards the lord, watching over his shoulder to keep the worm the right distance behind him. He heard it breathing. He had never been so close to it before, or it had never been so close to him. Its sinuous progress was straightening out the faster it moved. He looked ahead, and drew a little to the right. He had to pass as close as possible to the lord, so that the worm confused the two of them and was not prepared for the sudden blow that came from the lord. The lord spurred forward and passed on Jackson's right, the lance no more than a foot from Jackson's shoulder. In this way he came outside Jackson and was up at the worm before it saw him and had the lance buried in its body at the base of the neck.

The worm checked at once, pivoting on the pierced place and bunching up the whole of its body. The lord had foreseen that this would happen, and as soon as the lance was in he had released it, and swung away to the left sharply. He rode round the tail of the beast and came round to the wood and took another lance. He waited. Jackson, when he had crossed the lord and seen the worm had checked, rode off the feeding ground and came to the wood in the same way.

The worm writhed and bellowed and turned its head to its shoulder, but was not able to get its mouth on to the lance. A green blood dripped on the ground.

"It's in too high," said the lord. "It went in well and there was no bone to turn it. I can't put another one in that side, or I'll run into that lance. I wonder whether spears would hinder it just as much, if I put them along its flank, down the same side. I may be able to weaken it and make it lift its body up so that I can get at its heart. Can you distract it again, Jackson?"

"As long as the horse can still outrun it," said Jackson.

They laid a plan again. The worm had halted where it had been struck, but in a little while it began to move as easily as ever, finding the horse's scent going round itself. It turned round in its own length, and the lord postponed the plan he had just made and rode out to jab two spears along its side just behind the protuberance. This checked the worm again, and it turned back to see what had happened to that other side. It drew the spears out with its mouth, took them in, and a moment later spat them out as two small spheres. Then it nuzzled the place where they had struck. It checked its search for the horse for a very short time, and began to seek again.

"Now," said the lord, when the creature was looking towards the wood where he was. Jackson rode out with the lord beside him, obscured from the worm's view by Jackson. The lord took up a stand again in the middle of the field, and Jackson repeated the earlier tactics. This time the lord struck the lance in further back, but he did not get away readily. The lance went in close in front of the rounded protuberance. As it went in the worm's body lifted along one side, and a winged claw unfolded from its side, and knocked over horse and man. The horse screamed. The man lay flat. The claw, which had been folded under the protuberance, flailed the air, and a pallid membrane opened and became stiff and translucent. The worm turned away from it for a moment, as if it were startled by its sudden appearance. Then it swung round again and saw the horse under the wing. The mouth closed on the horse and lifted it, crushed it, and dropped it. Under the coiling side the lord lay black and still. The worm laid its head on the horse and watched. Its body gathered up. Jackson saw that it was about to rest on the lord. He called the men out from the wood, and rode towards the worm himself.

Now there were many targets for it to choose from, and it was disinclined to leave its prey, though it was not eating it yet. Then it moved suddenly, flailing that wing again. Under it the lord had risen from the ground and was hacking with his sword, tearing the membrane, and chopping at the root.

The lord was not alone now, however. Three men had come to him and were pulling him away. Jackson was ten feet from the jaws of the thing, feeling its snowy breath. He blew the trumpet at it, and is responded with a cry and moved towards him.

Four men were crushed by it. It gathered up the bodies and made a heap of them beside the horse, because it had not followed Jackson more than fifty feet. It turned on itself and looked at its side, at the wounded winged claw. Then it bit at it and tore it off, and laid the tattered thing on the heap of dead.

It lay there, still but watchful, and the frost gathered against it. The men brought the lord round to the wood. His armour was yellowed and marked with little pits. They pushed his visor up and washed his face for him.

"I can still see," he said, though his skin was reddened and swollen round his eyes. The men who had brought him were worse hurt. Jackson sent them to wash in the river. They went and did not come back.

"The other horse," said the lord. "Mount me on it. I shall go out alone now, and either win or lose, and no attempt must be made to help me. If there is anything left bury me in the courtyard."

Then he rode out in full fury, placed a lance on the left side of the worm, dismounted and sent his horse back and attacked with his sword, hacking at the head, trying to cut it off.

The worm screamed, had a sudden enormous convulsion, rose some way into the air on one unfolded wing from its left side, scoured its way round the feeding ground with all its known energy, and went back to its lair, calling as it went.

They found the lord in a pool of slime. He was dead and worse than dead. When they moved the armour his dissolved substance ran out of the joints, so they let it drain until the drainings froze, and took the lightened metal that had contained him back to the wood, and strapped the suit to a post from the palisade, and carried it back into the town and into the castle yard. Far away the worm howled. Overhead the sky grew down to night.

And throbbed, and grew smaller, and there was movement. Donald was sitting opposite Berry in a train. He had a sense of coming only now to actuality in being with Berry, though he could remember what had gone before; how Berry had given him coffee, and brought him to the station, and now had been talking for some time about the Tobies and why they were still at home, and Donald knew he had answered, but had been somewhere else as well.

"You look better," said Berry. But Donald felt more desolate than he ever had before. His mind, and the world, were both empty of meaning. The day was happening not only without him, but in a quite different dimension.

X

THE DAY WAS a strange numb drag. Berry took him to another town, whose name and position he was hardly aware of, and they had lunch. Then they went to speak to a retiring clergyman in a stuffy rectory and met people meaningless to Donald in a parish hall close by a main road. Donald was looking for peace and inactivity and the opportunity to become invisible to the world. He found it here, neglected in this meeting for nearly an hour, and was reluctant to move when the time came for them to leave. He followed dumbly behind Berry back to the railway station and sat in the train again, not miserable, but unworking. Berry was not quite pleased with him, he knew, but Berry was part of the dead world he looked out on. Berry looked out of the window and started a conversation. Donald could not think of anything to say at all, and was not able to reply.

"Let's be clear," said Berry. "Have I done anything to offend you, or are you sulking, or are you depressed?"

"None of those things," said Donald. "Nothing's real, that's all, but I keep knowing it's all there is but getting a feeling that there's something else. If I could find it."

"Physically, or religiously?" said Berry. "Or a mixture?"

"Mentally," said Donald. "If it would only come to me."

"We're alone," said Berry. "Talk about it. I'm a priest, and if it were of a confessional nature, or any nature at all, I would not be able to repeat it. Nor would I be shocked."

"There isn't anything," said Donald. "But I wish it would go away."

The train flapped into a tunnel and shook, then there was a settling into stillness, and a change of light, and Jackson was looking at a bloated, wounded man in the infirmary. Carrica was there, tending him. She was sponging his skin with milk.

"We have used it before," she said, because Jackson had asked whether it was a good treatment. Then she put milk on his hands too, because they were seared by the slime of the worm.

In the yard Miral was digging a hole. In the hole would go the armour they dared not look inside. Outside the gates a silent gathering waited, without knowing what for. Up in the valley the worm called regularly. Two of the elders had come to the castle and wanted to speak to Jackson, but he was having his hands seen to first.

"When I first came," he said, "do you remember what you said to me, down by the river."

"I said the new lord would be killed by the worm," said Carrica. "I was right, at last. But I was most frightened because he took you to be his boy, and I thought it might mean you would be killed with him. I was wrong there."

"There is time for me to be killed," said Jackson. "Now I am a knight I am able to challenge the worm if I wish, and if I do, and if I win, then there is the fee standing in the chest. And the council, in the end, would make me a full knight."

"Then you will go," said Carrica. "Shall I call you sir?"

"I shall not be lord in this town," said Jackson. "You may not call me sir, because we were children together."

"For a day," said Carrica. "You are a man now, and I am a woman. I am humble still, but you are of rank."

"I will get myself a name," said Jackson. "But I shall not bother to do it yet. Carrica, I cannot come here again tonight, because there are duties within the castle, and elders to speak to. And there is another duty outside the town."

"If you come back from them all," said Carrica, "perhaps we shall speak again."

"Yes," said Jackson, and he went out of the infirmary.

The elders were troubled by the howling of the worm. They were sure that the noise would bring others of the breed to it.

"I shall go at first light," said Jackson. "What else can I do? There is no one else of sufficient rank to fight the worm, and I have no skill or knowledge of fighting. When I am dead, and if there is anything left, put me beside the lord."

"You will be killed," said one of the elders. "And we shall not send you any men to help, because they will be killed too. The people think that they should take their goods and leave this place for ever."

"The worm would follow," said Jackson. "Here we have the town wall. Out on the road there is nothing."

Jackson spent the night without sleep. He thought he would be dead before he tired. Twice he went out on horseback with Miral, to see what the worm was doing. The first time the worm was in its lair, but the second time it had been down to the feeding ground and eaten its own wing and the dead horse, stiff in cold, and then roved the hill. They saw it moving from the far side. It seemed to have no hurt.

Before he went out Jackson spoke to Miral. "You are descended from the lords of this town," he said. "When I am dead, which will be very soon, you will act as lord. I cannot tell you how to deal with the worm before it takes the whole town. But watch what I do and do not follow my mistakes."

Then he went out alone, on his own horse, with a lance and his sword. He had no armour. At the feeding ground he blew the trumpet, and waited. The worm came. He had no helper and no tactics. He charged as soon as he was seen, swerved away from the opened mouth with its barrel-vault of teeth and its tongue of the same. The lance hit, but not a straight blow. It broke the skin but did not go deeply in, only running along just below the surface. The side of the creature was at that moment lifting in one of its contractions. The lance point was dragged upwards, the end he held was forced down, he was pulled from the horse and rolled on the ground with one foot still in the stirrup. The horse ran away with him, but not very far. The head of the worm came round and took it in among the grinding teeth. Jackson was dropped. The stirrup leather snapped, because the teeth had touched it, and he lay on the ground, unregarded. He put his hand to his sword, but the sheath was empty. The sword had fallen away and he could not see it. He had nothing to fight with.

He ran away. The worm, toying with the horse, did not see him or perhaps did not need him. He ran to the wood, and considered what to do next. The worm threw the horse aside and then began to scan with its head. Jackson saw it settle its look in his direction, and hunch itself like a cat. Then it did what he had never seen it do before. It sprang into the air and forward, propelled by a movement of its tail that scooped out a great spray of earth. At the top of its leap it attempted to fly. The left-hand wing came out and held the air, but the right-hand one was missing. The great blue pulsing stain of the heart showed against its belly. The creature coiled in the air, vainly, and fell to the ground. The ground shook. The worm climbed and squirmed in itself and came the right way up. The extended wing folded shut with a dry rustle and was stowed beneath its cover. Then its head sought again, and fixed once more on Jackson.

This time he did not wait for it. He turned and ran deeper into the wood and up the hill and then down the valley and slightly down the hillside. He had gone before the worm found his place again. He heard it call and ran faster, stumbling and grasping the ground itself to help himself along. But the voice of the worm had come no nearer. It was still at the feeding ground. It called again, and he began to run less fast. His lungs were sharpened and raw with exertion and the effect of the worm's exudation, but he had to breathe fast. He sat down and thought he would die there, because breathing afforded him no relief, and he wanted more air than he could get. Then he began to cough a moist cough, and a clammy faintness came on him, and a darkness he could not fight off.

It was dark when he woke, breathing more easily. He could hear nothing, and smell no fresh worm smell. He looked about and knew where he was in the valley. Not far below was the shuttered town. He stood up and made a dizzy journey to it, coming at last to the north gate. He kicked the gate and shouted as much as he could, but shouting brought on the moist cough and faintness again. No one heard, no response came from within. The gates were never opened after dark. He leaned against the gate and waited all night, not awake and not asleep. There was nothing else to do, unless he came up through the river gate, and the thought of that journey was too much for him. He leaned where he was.

Berry woke him from a thick-headed train sleep when they were coming into the station. He got up, and walked feeling as if he were a little behind himself, along the platform.

"Well now," said Berry, "that little outing has done nothing for you, Donald. I think you are acting in an unfriendly way, and I don't know why. But I'll walk with you up to the hospital and see whether your mother is there."

"I don't want to go in with you," said Donald.

"I can go in without you," said Berry. "Or you can go in without me, whatever you like. You're not responding like your usual self, so I'll humour you."

"It's all me," said Donald. "Nothing's right."

"I'm sorry," said Berry. "I'm not being helpful. There's a lot that isn't right, I know."

More than you know, thought Donald. Who am I, who are you? Are you the man lying in the bed? Is the man in the bed you? Who is my mother? Where did I come from? But the questions would not arrange themselves sensibly, askably.

Berry went into the hospital. Donald stood outside, leaning by the side of the door. Berry came out again and said, "I'm going to catch the next bus, but your mother will be down soon."

"Thank you for taking me," said Donald, and wished the words had meaning, that Berry was not another empty person in a sharply-seen but fragile world.

"I haven't done as much for you as I ought," said Berry,

putting his hands on Donald's shoulders. "I wish I could wait longer, but there's a meeting tonight."

He went. Donald leaned against the doorway again. Somewhere in the building he was touching lay another life that was linked to his. Between them there should have been some sort of electric current, but instead there was an insulating block, and no flow at all.

Mrs Jackson was down in half an hour. "We'd better hurry," was her greeting, and they hurried to the bus. "There's an improvement," she said. "He moved his legs just a little. Donald, he moved his legs. But I'll tell you when we get home. I'm much too tired now."

She was still tired when they got home. Donald felt neither tired nor awake, and watched himself lighting the fire. Then, when the fire was burning, Mrs Ross came to the door, bringing teacakes and toasting them under the grill and doing all the talking for the first half hour. With the warmth of the fire outside him and the comfort of familiar food inside, Donald felt the world become its own size again, and of an inhabitable nature, with all its parts as he had known them, the room and the house beyond the room his own place. Nothing else need be thought of for the time being.

"I can tell it's not so bad," said Mrs Ross. "Though you look quite tired out, both of you."

"It's hopeful," said Mrs Jackson. "If the doctors would realize that it's not in their hands it might be more hopeful still. He managed to move his legs this afternoon."

"That's news," said Mrs Ross. "You must be glad."

"There was never much wrong physically," said Mrs Jackson. "We knew it was a visitation from God."

"Such things are not unknown," said Mrs Ross.

"And we never grudged the visitation," said Mrs Jackson. "It was put upon us for our own good."

"But what do the doctors say?" said Mrs Ross.

"We don't know that," said Mrs Jackson. "We never know that. But his pain has gone, and he wants to come home as soon as he can."

"He has strength," said Mrs Ross. "When will it be?"

"Not tomorrow," said Mrs Jackson. "But as soon as possible. Perhaps by the week end. He's had a little fever, you know, and we want that to clear."

They talked of fevers. Donald went to bed. Before he slept he heard Mrs Jackson humming to herself as she washed up.

In the morning he went to school. Mrs Jackson did not suggest taking him to the hospital again so he had no decision to make. In the evening he was walking home alone, after walking part of the way with Nessing. He was halfway up Hales Hill when the town gates opened just after dawn and the labourers came out to go to the county fields on the north side. Jackson waited for them to go past and then went into the town.

He was not looked at or greeted. He wondered why for a time, until he looked at his sleeve, that should have been red cloth. It was patched dark with the stains of the hillside, and whitened by the worm, and torn. His sword belt was no longer round his hips, and his skin was dirty and swollen where it was stung by contact with the venom.

Then he was recognized by someone unknown, and there was a shout that was not friendly. He was too weary now to turn and speak, though he knew that as a knight and the acting lord he should rebuke insolent speech. He walked on up the hill.

He came along the street past the infirmary, going towards the castle gate. There were hurrying feet behind him, and a clean hand lay on his fouled sleeve. It was Carrica's hand.

"Come away," she said. "I do not care what you did."

"I don't know what I did," said Jackson. "I will come to the infirmary later. I must go to the castle now and fill the record books."

"Not with that," said Carrica. "Not with that."

"With what?" said Jackson.

"You ran away," said Carrica. "And I'm glad you did."

"Of course I ran away,' said Donald. "There was nothing else to do."

"But you are a knight," said Carrica. "And a knight will never run away when combat has been joined."

"The combat is not over," said Jackson, and he walked on. The battle could start again that day, or another day. A battle had been lost, but not a war, he thought.

There were elders in the castle yard, with Miral. They looked at him, and knew him, but they did not speak. Always before they had spoken with him.

"Sir knight," said one of them, "you may not come in here."

"I am the lord for now," said Jackson.

"You are the knight that broke combat," said the elder. "You are the same as a dead man to us, but not dead as he is," and he pointed to the mound where the lord lay. "You are living, but dead to all men. You were a knight, and you fled from the battle. There are two ways to leave combat, victorious or dead, or left for dead by the enemy. But you ran away. You are not a victor. You are one of the dead."

"If you were still a squire," said another elder, "then there would be no disgrace. And no town may take a disgraced knight in, so that you must leave. It would have been better if you had not come in, because now you will have to go out through the people, and there is no law to protect you. You are out of grace. You may not reach the gate alive, Jackson."

"He will reach the gate alive," said Miral. "Jackson and I have fought many fights, and I can fight for him now instead of against him. Which way will you leave, Jackson?"

"By the south gate, Miral," said Jackson.

"You must call me squire," said Miral. Jackson bowed his head.

"First I will write in the book what I have done," he said.

"No," said Miral. "Leave the last page open at a noble death, not at a cowardly shame."

Then he notioned Jackson to follow him and they went out of the gate into the street again.

"Go into the infirmary," said Miral. "Quick, lad."

Jackson stepped into the entry across the street and Miral stepped after him. "I can do nothing for you," said Miral. "I would if I could, but you have done a wrong thing and no one can protect you. All I can do is give you better clothes, and I will say I took away the lord's tunic."

Carrica came out of the inner room, carrying a bowl and a cloth. "I said it was not right to go in," she whispered, because Miral had spoken in a low voice. Then she washed his face and his feet and brought him a plain tunic.

"Come now," said Miral.

"Wait in the lord's fields," said Carrica. "I can bring you bread." And that was all the farewell he could take, because Miral was beckoning him. He went out of the infirmary, and Miral walked beside him down to the south gate, and then a little way beyond.

"That is it, then," said Miral. "Your time here is over."

Jackson walked out of the valley, up on to the hillside where the lord's fields were, that had been his fields for so short a time, and on to the sunny hilltop, and sat against a broken wall and slept.

"Donald," said Mrs Jackson, "you must have been dreaming not to have heard me come in." She was standing in the doorway of his room, and he was working at his homework, remembering what he had done since coming home without feeling he had experienced it.

"I don't think I heard," he said. "Sorry."

"He's coming home in the morning," said Mrs Jackson. "He feels he would be more comfortable here, and I think I can manage, because all he has to do is rest now, and the district nurse will come in each day, and they are thinking of some exercises for his legs."

"I'll put the kettle on," said Donald. He thought there was a brittle, desperate quality about Mrs Jackson's words. He felt that she was only pretending to believe about the legs. Perhaps she was thinking that if he could move his legs he would be easier to nurse.

Mrs Ross came in again, and this time the talking was not only round the kitchen fire but in the bedroom as well, where a sudden big cleaning was done, and the bed remade. Mrs Ross took away the curtains from that room, and promised to bring them first thing in the morning. When Donald went to bed the kitchen was being dealt with.

"It's a relief," said Mrs Jackson, "to have something to do and a reason for doing it. Donald will be glad to have his father back again. He was so shy of visiting him in the ward with all the other people there."

"They get so self-conscious at that age," said Mrs Ross. "Oh, my dear, there's been a mouse, did you know?"

XI

THE NEXT DAY was Saturday. When Donald woke he thought, first, that there was no need to stir because there was no school, and next that there was no bus to catch, and then that Daddy was coming home. He sat up when he thought that and thought of the bed in the other room being occupied, and heaviness came on him.

Mrs Jackson was already up. Donald stayed where he was, not wanting to join in the movement in the rest of the house, not wanting to be part of a welcome he could not feel. Mrs Jackson looked in and said she was going shopping, it was quarter past nine, and the ambulance was expected at ten. Donald got up and had his breakfast while she was gone, and washed the dishes he had used. He went outside and looked at the drive. More leaves had fallen on it and he swept them up. Then he moved the drift of them that had got on to the car, and swept away the webs of spiders that had grown on the windscreen wipers and over the controls inside the car. He slid the window shut. Mrs Jackson came back, put away her shopping, and they waited. Mrs Ross came over with the curtains and helped hang them, but Mrs Jackson said that, though she was glad to see her, perhaps Mr Jackson would be a little tired after his journey, and could she come another time and not wait now. Mrs

Ross said she understood perfectly, and went away without being offended.

Just after ten o'clock the ambulance cast a creamy light into the house, and the hedge cast a greenish light on the side of the ambulance. It moved about in the road, and backed into the drive and stood still. Mrs Jackson opened the door of the house, and the attendant opened the back of the ambulance. The driver got out and came to Mrs Jackson.

"He hasn't travelled too well," he said. "But he insisted on coming the whole way. They shouldn't have sent him out, we think."

"He will be happier here," said Mrs Jackson, smiling and happy herself.

Mr Jackson lay still and pale on his stretcher. One hand lay cold and still on his chest. His mouth was open and he breathed shallowly. Donald stood in the kitchen and watched him being taken through to the bedroom, feeling a numb terror at the presence of illness, and seeing too that the movement of one of Mr Jackson's legs was not anything he could help or control but a spasmodic twitching. As soon as he had gone through Donald went out of the house and into the garden. He heard the ambulance doors close and the motor start, and Mrs Jackson came out and called to him.

"You can come in now," she said. He came out of the garden, hoping to find some consolation with her, but there was none. Her own smile had gone. "Don't go through," she said. "He wants some time to settle, I expect. Perhaps you'll run down to Dr Riley's and tell him Daddy's back. There's a letter for him from the hospital."

"Run?" said Donald.

"I don't mean run," said Mrs Jackson. "Walk will do, but telephoning won't, because of the letter." She had the letter in her hand, and wanted to open it, but it was addressed to Dr Riley. "What does it say?" she said, fingering it and feeling the folded paper inside.

Donald put the letter in his pocket and went out again, down the hill, away from the house. Mr Jackson had come back, but that had resolved nothing, he found. No sudden balance of feeling or easing of tension had come with him. Instead the whole life of the house, the whole intent of the day, seemed to centre on him, or on something near him, his illness.

He walked along beside a warm wall, looking at the ground, more and more slowly until he stood still, with the sun touching his neck. Ahead of him there was the noise of someone walking, and he saw bare feet coming through the grass. It was Carrica, and he was not in Hales Hill but on another hill, against a field wall.

"I came out with some food for you," she said.

"I have nothing for you," he said. "I am disgraced."

"I know," said Carrica. "But you helped me once, and I will help you now."

Jackson was hungry. He ate bread and cheese and drank water, because there was clean water in a stream.

"You tried to do more than you could manage," said Carrica. "You were braver than the lord. You went out without any armour."

"I had no armour," said Jackson. "And I might not have used it if there had been any. You do not know what happened to the lord in his armour. There is no rule of armour, only a rule of combat."

"It is no disgrace, *I* think, to leave a battle when you have no weapon left," said Carrica.

"I did not behave properly," said Jackson. "I was frightened, and I ran away. The lord taught me the rules of combat, and showed me how to fight the worm. I challenged it, and attacked it, and when I was beaten I should have died, and they would be remembering me differently now."

"I would rather see you," said Carrica, "than remember you in any way at all."

"Now I cannot kill the worm honourably," said Jackson. "There is no honour left in me."

"There are other ways," said Carrica. "The way of honour has killed the lord, and it has made you dead. I do not kill flies with honour. I hit them with a stone."

"If I killed the worm in any other way than by battle I should not bring honour to myself," said Jackson. "And since I have no honour I cannot challenge it. But there is a way to kill it."

"Kill it, then," said Carrica. "With a stone, perhaps. I shall go now, but I shall come back here for three days, and if you are not here I shall remember you."

"I shall be here if I can be," said Jackson. Carrica gathered up her basket and went back into the fields on her way to the town. Jackson sat down and thought.

The lord had made him think first of honour and order and the accepted way of doing things. His own life had been one of observation, assessment and regulation. The orderliness had at last killed him, because the accepted way of dealing with worms had been fatal. Some other attack would be more successful. To a squire, a knight, or a lord, or to the council that

133

Jackson had heard of, only the honourable way could be thought of, the open confrontation, the hopeless attack against the venomed front of a mighty beast. But there must be other ways.

In the middle of the day Jackson left the fields and walked along the ridge of the hill, going inland until he was beyond the town and opposite the feeding ground. He crossed the worm track, unused for several days, and came down to the river. There was no sign of the worm, no sound or smell. He crossed the river, and the cold water bit under the reddened skin. He came up to the feeding ground and trod in yesterday's acid slime once more, and cried out with the pain. On the ground, after a long search, he found his sword, and near it the trumpet. He took them both to the river and washed them. Then he came up to the wood and found another thing he would need, a woodman's axe, used for making the palisades. With these he was ready. He stood at the edge of the woods and blew the trumpet.

The worm answered. He knew it would come. He ran away again, but this time towards the lair of the worm, staying up on the hill. He saw the worm pass by lower down.

He came to its lair. He had never been right up to it, but he had observed it often. He had the sword naked, because sheath and belt were both lost. He came across rocks and on to the grey ice, and to the central road that the creature had made in its entrance and exit from the lair.

The road was slippery. When he first trod in it he went down head over heels, with the sword and axe running beside him, and landed at the bottom bruised and bleeding. He climbed the chute again by hacking footholds as he went, and the broken ice scattered and tinkled as it went down behind him. Half way up he stopped and began to dig a hole wide enough for himself. The ice chipped off in small pieces, and he had to throw them out by hand. But he was down two feet before he heard the worm returning slowly. It bellowed once, and he thought he had been seen. He climbed out of the chute and went among the rocks. The worm did not look about, but slid its length up the chute, ignoring the hole, writhed inside its lair, and was still.

Jackson rested until it must be asleep. Then he left the sword and the axe and went back to the feeding ground and called it out again, and again it came.

This time he set to work as soon as he got there, without tumbling down the slide. The worm did not soon come back. He heard it far away calling, and, looking round once, saw it on the track below the lord's fields.

Before it came back he had made a hole deep enough to crouch in, and could not go much further because he had come upon the underlying rock. The worm came back, and he hid again, going well up the hill and resting in the sunshine, trying to wipe off as much of the filth and slime as he could.

He waited for the night, and slept. Then waking at twilight, he stood up where he was and blew the horn again, sure that the worm would not go anywhere but to the feeding ground.

The twilight turned to the internal glittering of sunshine on the decorated glass of the doctor's house next door. Donald rang the bell, and the doctor came. Donald gave him the letter from the hospital. He read it, said "Hmn," in a dissatisfied way, and said he would be along as soon as possible.

135

Donald walked back home with that message. Mrs Jackson was sittting with Mr Jackson. She heard him come in and called to him, and he had to go into the room. Mr Jackson looked at him and said, "Donald," in a voice that was half question. Donald looked at him and looked away. He gave Mrs Jackson the message and went out of the room, because it was unbearable to be in that presence. He went out again, into the road and looked at nothing. He knew that what he felt was unaccountable and wrong, that he should be in the house and not looking for reasons to be out of it, for reasons to fly from Mr Jackson. But there was something that he did not want to be with, that he could not bear the thought of, and he did not know what it was.

He stirred from his mood of standing still, and thought of a place to go, and went quickly to the vicarage to see Berry. He knew that was wrong too, and that Mr Jackson would not like it, and that Berry was busy on Saturdays with his sermons.

He was busy, but the busyness made it more urgent for Donald to see him. Berry was not quite glad to see him, and that seemed to Donald to be the last rejection possible. He had let his own home reject him, and now he had no shelter. Berry sat him on a sofa and waited for him to state his needs and be gone. But there were no needs he could state. He sat and looked at Berry, and then, suddenly, was in tears.

"How, now," said Berry. "What happened?"

"Nothing," said Donald. "Daddy's come back, and I can't bear it." Berry abandoned his sermons and sat beside Donald. He shouted through to his wife to bring coffee and take the Tobies away.

Donald burnt his lips on the coffee, and it made him feel

sick. But he managed to stop crying and feel sensible but not calm.

"You can sit here and talk," said Berry. "Or you can sit here and I'll do my sermons, or I'll sit here and you can do the sermons. I don't mind which."

"I'll talk," said Donald, and then said nothing for about a quarter of an hour. Berry sat patiently beside him with an arm round his shoulders.

"What is it in the end?" he said.

"I haven't any fatherly feelings towards him," said Donald at last, and cried again.

"They wear off," said Berry. "When I was about fifteen I despised my father."

"No," said Donald. Berry went on.

"I was secretly against him until I was twenty. Then I was more tolerant and put up with him. Then, when I was about thirty I was far enough away to see him as a separate person without being too much entangled in the relationship. Now that I'm forty-four I think of him as a jolly old cove who's been much the same all his life, a practising pagan and a Christian old gentleman. As I get older I get more like him, a practising Christian and a pagan old gentleman. What I mostly despised in him was what I saw in myself, or suspected I saw, or sometimes what I thought other people might see."

"He used to make racing car noises," said Donald. "But now he doesn't do anything."

"He has a lot of physical stress," said Berry. "Do you know that I am to blame?"

"No," said Donald. "How?"

"I was a zealous young priest," said Berry. "When I came

137

here I only thought of adding to the number of people at the church. I was foolish. I used to convert them from their own religions to my own church. I sent your sister Cecily to the bishop to be confirmed. It was on the way back from the service in the city that the accident happened."

"The railway accident," said Donald.

"Yes," said Berry. "Cecily was killed, your father was hurt as he is now. And it was worse because your parents did not want her to join my church at all. But she was a very determined girl, and she persuaded them to allow it. They even agreed that she should go to the bishop a month early, in town, instead of waiting until he came here—you were due to be born, you see. As it happened, you were born the night of the accident, a month early. It was shock, you see. I don't think they've ever quite forgiven you for not being Cecily again."

"They liked her best," said Donald. "Did you like her?"

"I like you better," said Berry. "But that's not the point, is it?"

"I don't like him," said Donald. "It's wrong, even if you say it isn't."

"It's an uncomfortable state," said Berry. "They have not liked me since then, not because of the accident, but because of Cecily. He gave all the compensation money to the chapel, you know, and did not use any for the proper purpose, making it easier for him to live, and easier for you. He's a very firm, hard man, of strict principles. You need not like him, Donald, but you must attempt to love him. Now sit there and practise loving while I do some more at my sermons. Thank goodness I shall have a big stock of them laid by for the next place. They haven't listened to them there yet."

Donald went on sitting on the sofa. What they had been talking about was not what pressed on him most. He thought he could see all the people around him and found they were all in the wrong places. He needed a place to see them from so that they were all in their right order. Somewhere, he thought, there is a place that is right for me, there is a way of looking at things, and a time when the world will run smoothly again. But he could not see that time coming.

Berry wrote, and looked up and smiled, and wrote again. Mrs Braxham came in and said lunch was ready. Donald got up to go, but they asked him to stay as long as he liked.

"I'll not be here much longer to be unpopular," said Berry.

Perhaps that was it, thought Donald. There is coming a time soon when there will only be the man in the bed, and this one, who means more to me, will have gone away.

In the afternoon he went home. "Be of good courage," said Berry. "Traditional advice but good. Look forward to better things when he is well again."

Mrs Jackson was asleep in the kitchen. Donald let himself in and watched the sunlight dancing on the moving dust. Mrs Jackson opened her eyes and closed them again and murmured something, but was asleep at once. From the bedroom came quick, noisy breathing. Donald went into his own room and settled to his week-end homework.

Teatime came, and that breathing went on. Mrs Jackson did not ask him where he had been for lunch. He wanted to go out again, to escape, but this time he would have to ask, and he did not like to display in words his desire to be out of the house. He stayed in.

Mrs Ross came in, and she and Mrs Jackson talked quietly.

Donald stayed in the room reading, and then went to bed, and lay a long time without sleeping. Once he woke in the night and, terrified, heard a meaningless conversation, one side composed of words that were moans, and the other Mrs Jackson replying soothingly. The shallow breathing continued.

It was early morning. Donald woke and sat up, and still the lungs across the passage rasped and fluttered. Donald's back was cold. He put his jacket round it and leaned on the wall.

His feet were cold. The ice was settling its chill on him. Jackson scraped away at the rocky earth underfoot and found himself a few more inches. He did not throw the earth into the chute because the worm might see it as it came back. He heard it bellow from not far away, approaching from a fruitless search at the feeding ground. Jackson laid the axe aside and crouched low. He gripped the sword in both hands, and waited. The sword pointed up to the misty sky, the point just below the edge of the hole he had dug and was now crouching in.

There was a quavering of the ground, not felt by his frozen feet but perceived in his gut. His heart began to race and icicles grew from his armpits, icicles or very cold sweat. He bent his head low and waited.

The ice shook. The worm was on the chute. Then darkness surged over his head and he could see nothing and could not tell which way was up or down. But over him, beyond his head, ruffling his hair, was the belly of the worm, and in that belly was the blue pulse that was the heart. The worm paused. He had seen it do that before. Above him there was a moist thud, the beating of that heart, and he felt the belly wall of the creature stretch at the beat of the heart. He tightened his jaw and every muscle and plunged the sword upwards.

There was a blind convulsion. The sword was torn from his hands and he was pulled from the hole because he went on gripping. His hands were cut but numbed. Then he fell to the ground, down into the chute again. The chute was empty. There was a huge yell in the air, and towering above him the worm standing on its tail, taller than the castle tower. Up on the side of this tower there was a patch of colour, just visible in the twilight, and in that colour stood the sword.

The creature toppled, falling in a coil, then rebounding from the earth and straightening, and rolling on to its back. From it came a last titanic yelp, and then it subsided into a stillness and moved no more.

Jackson stood up, and then knelt, because of the dizziness that came over him. In a little while he walked over to the dead creature and stood beside it. It was slain in unfair combat, and no glory from its death could come to him. He had accomplished no duty. He was not restored to honour.

He went out of that place, down to the river, and washed himself. Then he walked up the further hillside until he came to the lord's fields and found the wall he had been at this morning. He lay there in the clearer hill air and slept.

At dawn he woke to a golden sky lifting from the sea. He looked down towards the town, and saw there, for the first time, the sunlight touching the tower of the castle. The bank of mist brought by the worm had vanished with the light. He got up stiffly and walked along the hillside, until he could look down on the unmoving beast in the bottom of the valley.

Then he came back to where he had been, and waited.

He was now in two worlds. One of them was the hillside and the green grass. The other was the house in Hales Hill, and the bed he had slept in and the thin wall he leaned against there, and both were actual, and he could choose which to be in. One was silent, and in the other the dreadful breathing continued. There was movement in the house. Mrs Jackson came through from the kitchen and went into the other room. In the other world there was movement too, and Carrica came up to him and found him. She knelt beside him and took his hands.

"I did it," said Jackson, but the boy in bed said nothing and only listened across the narrow passage.

"Come back to the town," said Carrica.

"No," said Jackson.

"They will come for you," said Carrica. "They have been up the valley and seen your sword in it."

"It was not an honourable deed," said Jackson. "It could not be."

Half of him watched the house in Hales Hill. Half looked at the girl, Carrica, the girl in the photograph. Carrica was not his. She was his mother or his sister, and of those two he knew which was which, and he knew that the man in the other room was his father, whom he knew now how to love. Carrica was a phantom if he wanted her to be, and the house in Hales Hill was another, and he had the choice of which to remain with.

In Hales Hill the sick man said "Open the curtains. I want to see the day." The curtains rattled open on their runners.

"I must go," said Jackson. "I shall start again in another place. I have not done well in this one."

Mr Jackson spoke. "Lord, now lettest thou thy servant," he said, and then was silent.

"I am going too," said Jackson, and he withdrew from the presence of Carrica, so that there was no more the sight of the lord's fields or the town beyond or that golden morning, but only the golden morning at Hales Hill, where reality was.

In the other room the curtains were closed again. Mrs Jackson came out of the room and closed the door and went into the kitchen. There was no more breathing. Donald lay and listened to the quiet, and went to sleep, consolate.